BOX HILL

Adam Mars-Jones

BOX HILL

A STORY OF LOW SELF-ESTEEM

A NEW DIRECTIONS PAPERBOOK ORIGINAL

First published in Great Britain by Fitzcarraldo Editions in 2020

Manufactured in the United States of America
First published as New Directions Paperbook 1485 in 2020

Library of Congress Cataloging-in-Publication Data
Names: Mars-Jones, Adam, 1954– author.
Title: Box Hill : a story of low self-esteem / Adam Mars-Jones.
Description: First New Directions edition. |
New York : New Directions Publishing, 2020.
Identifiers: LCCN 2020021802 | ISBN 9780811230056 (paperback) |
ISBN 9780811230063 (ebook)
Subjects: GSAFD: Bildungsromans.
Classification: LCC PR6063.A659 B69 2020 | DDC 823/.914—dc23
LC record available at https://lccn.loc.gov/2020021802

2 4 6 8 10 9 7 5 3 1

New Directions Books are published for James Laughlin
by New Directions Publishing Corporation
80 Eighth Avenue, New York 10011

BOX HILL

BOX HILL WHERE THE BIKERS GO, on a Sunday. Box Hill near Leatherhead in Surrey—jewel of the North Downs, rising almost four hundred feet sheer above the river (that's the river Mole). A cliff densely covered with box and yew. It's the steepness of the gradient means only box and yew can get a foothold. It could just as easily be called Yew Hill as Box Hill, except box trees are so much rarer.

Box is the heaviest European wood. It doesn't float. The roots were traditionally used for knife handles. Box trees are poisonous, same as yews. Only camels will eat the leaves, not because they're immune but because they're stupid, they don't know what they're doing. Box trees are used for mazes because the foliage is so dense, and they can be trained all the way down to the ground. A maze isn't much cop if you can lie down on your belly, see where you are and wriggle out of it.

The leaves of the box are ovate, entire, smooth, thick, coriaceous and dark green. I looked that up. It sounds like a poem you can't quite get the sense out of.

At Box Hill there's downland grazed by sheep. A rich chalk flora. Orchids for those who know them when they see them. It's a beauty spot overrun one day a week by motorcyclists and their beautiful machines. Bikes that whine, bikes that roar.

The Sunday of my eighteenth birthday: 1975. I went to look at the bikes. Because life at home wasn't much fun, just at that moment, with Mum in hospital and Dad being unlike himself. Because I was going to get a bike of my own, one day soon. Because I liked to look at the bikers. Because it was my birthday, and I didn't need a reason.

As far as riding my own machine, the closest I'd come to date was making the pilgrimage from Isleworth to Lewis Leathers in Great Portland Street, off Oxford Circus, to pick up a catalogue. Not very close. Tucked inside the catalogue was a leaflet telling you how to take your measurements for a one-piece suit. It had an outline of a human figure with arrows going this way and that, shoulder to wrist, inside leg.

I didn't think the one-piece suit idea was going to work. The outline didn't look much like me. A jacket in a standard size, once I could even afford that, would be a better bet. It would cover me up, though even so I wasn't sure. If it was big enough for me to get the zip done up over my tum, the sleeves would be much too long, and I'd be swimming inside the shoulders.

I fell over him. I tripped and fell over him. When he told people about how we met, Ray always made that clear: Colin didn't fall *for* me, he fell *over* me. Then he would continue the story with the bit that always made me uncomfortable. Ray would say, I took one look at him, and I saw what he really wanted.

I didn't think I knew what I wanted, and I'm still not sure why he chose me. I was never a looker. I never had a waist. But Ray was drop-dead gorgeous, though people didn't say that then. It wasn't a phrase. I didn't think Ray was drop-dead gorgeous in 1975. I was still reading teen magazines, and in 1975 the word in my mind was the word that teenagers used then. Ray was tasty.

I fell over him, just as he said. There's a side of Box Hill I call the shorn side, near the panorama, where the grass is short and neat, and this was the other side, where the grass is shaggy and not so tidied up. He was sitting against a tree with his eyes shut—not that I saw him—and his big feet crossed in front of him. It was the feet I fell over, the size twelves.

He was probably sleeping off a late night with a stomach full of fry-up from the café at the bottom of the hill, where everybody was wearing leather but nobody wore their leather as well as he did. He was so used to being looked at that he didn't notice any more. It would have been just like him, the person I came to know, to sit there reading a book after he'd finished eating. Military history. Something about the ocean and its creatures. He's the only person I've ever seen who could turn a page wearing leather gloves and not fumble.

For heaven's sake, the man could shuffle and deal a pack of cards without taking his gloves off—even if that was a party trick, something done for a bet with his poker club. Supple dress gloves, not his bike gloves. When he got off his machine, he'd pull off the stiff bike gloves and fold them in his helmet, then pull out the thin dress ones from his jacket pocket. A hundred to one those dress gloves were Mayfair jobs, made to measure, for his fingers to fit them so snugly, all the way to the tips.

And in the moment between gloves, when his hands were naked, he would use the left one to sweep back the leading edge of his thick yellow hair in a single brisk gesture, much too decisive to seem like grooming. You could never think of that poised impatient movement of the hand as grooming, let alone preening. Hair that was never either lank or unruly, and never long enough at the front to count technically as a quiff.

When people stared at him, Ray ignored them, but he wasn't used to people paying no attention in the first place. When I woke him up by tripping over him, it stands to reason that I suffered more than he did from the upset of our meeting. I went sprawling and barked my knees, while the worst thing that happened to him was that one bike boot scuffed the other. From the way he scowled, though, that was serious enough. When I dusted myself off and sat up on my haunches, Ray was glaring down at me and snarling, "Why don't you look where you're fucking going?"

I may have got the "fucking" in the wrong place. He might have said, "Why don't you fucking look where you're going?" It's hard to be sure after all this time, but there was definitely a "fucking" in it. I wasn't used to being sworn at, and I know I flinched. I was scared but I didn't run away—not that running has ever been a strong suit. One leg always trails behind when I try.

I couldn't take my eyes off him, that much is true, but who could have in my place? He was like a glossy catalogue illustration from Lewis Leathers, and I expect I looked like a tired window display from the Burton's menswear shop, when they've tried lots of backdrops and lighting schemes and they still can't make people want the merchandise. My flares were timid—yes it's possible for flares to be timid. My brown leather jacket had exaggerated rounded lapels. Its zip was plastic rather than metal and it went straight down the middle, not at the sexy angle of the ones on bike jackets. Ray was six foot five and I was what I still am, five foot six. Even if I'd been taller I would have been at quite a disadvantage, looking up at a stranger scowling down.

Except that, the way he always told it, it wasn't his scowl I was looking at. But it was news to me when he said, "I get it. So this is what you're interested in?" His voice changed, it was menacing in a different way. Menacing in a way that promised something. As much lazy as angry, now. I hadn't even realized I wasn't looking at his face. Not that it wasn't a fine face, a strong face, a chiseled face. I just wasn't looking at it.

He was always a step ahead of me. Sometimes a whole flight of steps. Looking down on me from the top of a flight of steps, wearing no expression, just waiting to see if I had the courage to follow him. Sometimes ducking round the corner so I had to run to catch up, breathless and stumbling, afraid that if I lost sight of him it'd be for good.

He was wearing one-piece leathers, and now he reached up to the neck, where there was a sort of lateral strap across the zip, fastened with a popper. He unsnapped it, and flicked it open with a finger. I watched, not really taking it in, as he slowly pulled the zip down all the way, down as far as it would go.

If Ray was six foot five, then a zip running from his neck down to a point between his legs must have been about three foot long. A zip a yard long. A zip more than half as tall as I am. It made a sort of whirring noise. A purring noise. Ray had a trick to keep zips from sticking, though of course I didn't know that then. Every week he would rub the stump of a candle along the zips of all his leathers. Oil doesn't work so well on a zip. It has to be wax. Oil dries out but wax remains.

The friction of the slide as it united or separated the chains of teeth would liquefy the wax, to form a lubricating layer. Ray's zips always purred as he pulled them open or closed, maintaining an absolutely even pressure.

When the slide of Ray's zip passed his collarbone, I thought he would stop there and pull something out to show me—I didn't know what: a crucifix, a locket with a picture of his wife. When the zip was approaching his navel, gliding through its film of invisible wax, I could only think he was reaching for a knife, and that I would stay there humbly crouching while he carved me up. As the panels of leather were freed to slide apart, the gliding zip slowly uncovered two narrow zones of sweat-dampened fur, one on his breastbone and one below his navel.

I was sweating, too, with fear as well as the warmth of the day, but my sweat was no more than a waste product. His was a sheen on him, the finishing touch to beauty. A sort of elixir.

Then when his zip reached the end of his track, I had to admit to myself that there was nothing else he could possibly be reaching for but what he brought out, his cock and balls. He reached in and tugged out his balls with the greatest care, arranging them like rare fruit on a bowl, a sculpture in a gallery window. I expect he wanted me to notice the sheer extent of his scrotum, and the plump cushion it provided for a cock that was lazily swollen without troubling itself to stand up just yet. Lolling and waiting, to see if there was something worth its time.

I began to realize that Ray's one-piece wasn't quite like the one in the Lewis Leathers catalogue, where the zip stopped discreetly short, instead of going as Ray's did right to the central seam of the crotch, to make possible just this frank presentation of himself. So one of the first things I learned from Ray was that there are other places to get specialized motorcycle clothes than Lewis Leathers in Great Portland Street, off Oxford Circus.

If I had been more observant I would have noticed something else: that Ray's one-piece had a double zip, so that it would have been perfectly possible for him to expose his parts by working a zip up from the bottom and not down from the top. This was a design element borrowed from arctic clothing, for the benefit of those who need to take a leak in extreme conditions, uncovering as little flesh as possible to frost and blizzard.

It didn't occur to me as I cowered hungrily in front of Ray that his unzipping had an element to it of ritual or of theater. The absence of underwear announced not just experience but experience in the form that intoxicates. Not just experience but practice.

I was frozen in place, as if I really was exposed to a blizzard without the protection of arctic clothing. I couldn't move. I was very conscious of my own breathing, more dimly aware of the rural rustle nearby and the distant roaring of bikes. I knew now what I was expected to do, and I also knew that I wanted it, but I wasn't actually able to make a move. I couldn't do it. Not by myself.

So Ray took pity on me. With one hand he shielded his cock, so as to put his balls on display even more prominently. With the other hand he clicked his fingers and nodded, once. The click of his fingers was muffled and made more subtly authoritative by his gloves.

He was making things easy for me, finding a task that even an absolute beginner like me could hardly mess up. After I'd paid attention to his balls, he flipped his cock forward and clicked his fingers again. That second click of his fingers resounded in a space that was not the space around us. It resounded inside my head. I felt as if he had clicked his fingers in the deepest part of my thinking, producing a brain event like the one that triggers a fit. In people prone to fits.

He was very patient with me. Whenever I choked, he let me

recover with his gloved hand resting on my neck, before he pulled me forward again. If I'd seen any pornography at all in my life I might have realized that what was happening could only happen to the people in pornography. But I hadn't, so it must really be happening.

I gave no thought to the possibility of someone walking in on us in our shaggy glade. Perhaps Ray was equally forgetful, fully taken up with his sensations, biting his lip and so on, trying not to moan, but I don't flatter myself. Pleasure didn't make him moan. On special occasions, it's true, a hoarse kind of shout burst out of him, but that's not the same thing.

The Ray I came to know would be fully aware of somebody coming near, however engrossed in pleasure he might seem to be. He was quite capable of keeping his eyes closed until a passerby was too near to have any doubts about what was being done, then opening them, letting those dazzling blue eyes do their work while he drawled, "Do you mind? Can't you see we're busy?" Then in a lower tone: some people have no manners.

When he pulled back from me and started to zip himself up, he slipped his thumb behind the head of the zip to make sure of not catching any of the hairs on his groin and chest. There was no hurry in his movements, but then it took a lot to make him hurry. He might have heard somebody coming after all, and been wanting to spare me the embarrassment that bothered him so little. He almost seemed to seek it out, to show how little it meant to him.

I didn't know what was going on. I wondered if his stopping meant that I had passed some test. Or failed one. I didn't know if it would be rude to pick stray hairs off my tongue. I hadn't stood up since I had tripped over Ray in the first place, and though my knees were aching I wasn't sure that my legs would carry me. I was dazed, half by what I had done and half by what Ray was. I might never have stood up if he hadn't made it happen in the end, putting his hands under my arms and giving me a boost upwards until my legs remembered their business. I was amazed by how easily he did it. I've never been a lightweight. I hadn't learned about his strength and fitness then—except that they were written all over him—his wrestling and martial arts.

"I'm Ray," he said, resting his hands on my shoulders, and I was just about able to gasp out "Colin." He was so much taller than me that I felt I'd been looking up at the same angle since the moment I'd laid eyes on him, even when I was connected to him by that angry tube of flesh. Even then, while I was trying to give him pleasure, in that tangle of anxious wanting, I was gazing crazily upwards in pubic darkness, wanting to look into his eyes.

I was still shaky, and he was so solidly built that even with his hands resting on my shoulders he seemed to be pushing me down to the ground one more time. My knees buckled again, and we went through a ridiculous repetition of the previous maneuver—his hands moving instantly to my armpits to give support. Up, down. It was no longer my responsibility.

For the first time he came close to smiling at me, even if it was a bleak sort of smile, and he asked with a shake of his head, "What am I going to do with you?"

I know there are some questions that don't expect an answer, but I couldn't let this be one of them. "Whatever you want." I wasn't sure I'd managed to say it out loud so I said it again, just in case the first time was in my head, because this was my chance and I needed him to hear. "Whatever you want to do."

He said, "Is there someone you need to phone?" He didn't leave one of those meaningful pauses, the sort people in soap operas leave, to show that this is a significant moment. He came straight out with it. No hesitation. I still don't understand how anyone could be so decisive. Ray just made up his mind there and then.

I honestly didn't get it. "What, now?" I wasn't playing hard to get. I can't even imagine playing hard to get. I was just being slow, as usual.

"To say you won't be going to where you're meant to be." For the first time I noticed that he had a leather jacket with him as well as his one-piece. It was rolled up against the tree as a manly sort of cushion. Now he picked it up and slung it over his shoulder, using his thumb as the hook from which it hung.

Where I was meant to be, later on, was at home in Isleworth. My little Mum was in hospital and we didn't yet know what was wrong with her. Dad was very upset about it, but I didn't know if there was a medical reason for that. He always seemed embarrassed about questions of female health, which was mad seeing he was a pharmacist, but he was also eleven years older than Mum and a man of that generation. It was natural to him. Pharmacists aren't doctors, they just have to be able to read doctors' handwriting. They don't deal directly with people's bodies, and if they're shy and retiring to start with there's no necessary reason they can't stay that way.

Mum had only been in hospital a few days, but Dad had been rotten to live with since then. She ran the shop, worked the till, and dealt with most things apart from actually making up the prescriptions. But that wasn't what was bothering him, the running of the shop.

An eighteenth birthday didn't mean then what it means

now—it didn't mean that what I'd been doing with Ray was legal, or would have been if only we'd done it indoors and not on the shaggy side of Box Hill. But it meant that as of today I could vote, the next time there was voting to be done, and as an adult, an adult citizen, it seemed fair that I could decide what to do with the rest of my special day. I couldn't just stay out, though, without sending word. I told Ray I'd need to talk to Ted. We set off towards Box Hill village to find him. The actual village, where the pub was. I was sweaty, so I took off my jacket and tried to drape it over my shoulder from a thumb like Ray was doing, but either the jacket or the thumb wasn't up to the job, and it kept sliding off. So I bundled it up and tucked it awkwardly under one arm.

Ted had been my ride to Box Hill, a biker that the younger of my two sisters, that's Joyce, had broken up with. But somehow the family hadn't managed to get rid of him. He'd turn up at odd hours, and Mum would always give him something to eat, even if Joyce was doing her routine of looking straight through him, not looking up from her magazine when he stood up and said goodbye.

I hope Ted wasn't waiting for Joyce to change her mind. She's a great one for changing her mind, is Joyce, but one thing she never does is to change it back. Volunteering to take me to Box Hill, to give me a treat and look after me on my birthday, might get him in good with my Dad, but it wasn't going to cut any ice with Joyce. In any case, Ted might have thought he was pining for Joyce, but it was beginning to look like a straightforward sulk.

Ted was one of those steady drinkers who don't much show the effects. I'm not even sure he would have been able to control his machine if he was sober. People didn't take drink-driving very seriously then. People in general, I don't mean just bikers. On the other hand, the drinking hours were tightly restricted in those days, especially on a Sunday.

I wasn't at all a drinker, but when I was with my sisters' friends everything seemed to be governed by the two great shouts of "They're open!" and "Who's getting them in?" The five hours on a Sunday between afternoon closing and evening opening were desert hours for them, a nightmare of parching between the two bouts of authorized trough-wallowing.

I'd left Ted in the Hand in Hand on Box Hill Road towards Headley Reservoir before last orders at two, and I knew he'd be thinking of buying some cans so as to last through the dry middle of the day. That was his way. Then he'd start again at seven o'clock opening. I'd told him I was going for a walk, take a look-see. Apart from anything else, I was hungry, and I knew from experience that Ted only thought of eating when there was absolutely no more drink to be had. I hadn't been willing to wait, and I knew there was a Wimpy bar on the other side of the road, towards the panorama, where I could get a hamburger and a glass of lemonade.

I wasn't that keen on having Ted drive me home sloshed, which he wouldn't want to do till evening closing anyway, but back then I hadn't had a choice. And now I did.

When Ray and I found Ted outside the Hand in Hand, his bike was on its side stand and he was lying on it after a fashion, with his eyes closed and his feet up on the handle bars. A beer can was loosely held by one sleeping hand against his grubby T-shirt. Earlier in the day I might have thought he looked quite cool like that, even though he was sending out snores that had a little bit of burp in them every now and then.

I had a new standard of cool demeanor now, one that neither

burped nor snored. When he opened his eyes and saw Ray, Ted struggled to his feet. For a moment the bike wobbled on its stand, and I thought one of them was going to fall—maybe even both. I hope I wouldn't have laughed if that had happened, but my allegiance was no longer with him, and I couldn't have guaranteed it. Only the beer can fell to earth, and he shot it one agonized look. Though anyone who knew him would have realized that awake, asleep or in between his body didn't have the power to drop a container with any alcoholic liquid left in it.

Ted drew himself up to try and look taller. Ray made everyone want to be at their best, to live up to him. To come up to his level. I could only hope that Ted's eyes weren't following Ray's zip down his body, the way mine did if I didn't keep them under orders, to see that it carried on a few inches further than most people would have thought was strictly necessary. Luckily if Ted was looking anyone up and down it was me, and not Ray.

"What's up, kid?" he asked, in a flat tone of voice. I suppose he was waiting for clues, willing to acknowledge me if I was making impressive friends, but ready to disown me in a flash if I'd done something wrong.

I told him he didn't need to worry about giving me a ride home. He tried to sound sober despite his drinking, and parental although he didn't know how, and the net result was to make his voice unrecognizable. "I'm not worried," he growled carefully, "but there are people who will be. I hope you've thought of them." It was downright embarrassing to remember that I had wanted him as part of the family. God help me, I'd thought Joyce could do a lot worse. I'd thought she was being hard on him.

"Tell Dad I've met a friend and I'll be staying with him." Ray hadn't said in so many words that I'd be staying over, and I shot him an anxious glance, but he didn't react at all, so I got a little extra confidence from that. I introduced the two of them, and Ted made a bit of a mess of shaking hands. When his siesta had overtaken him, he'd still had the ring pull from his beer can wedged past the knuckle of his middle finger, right hand. With the little curl of soft metal still attached to the ring, it looked like a piece of costume jewelery or a down-and-out's rather pathetic knuckleduster.

Ted held out his hand to shake, and then noticed the ring. He pulled abruptly back to wrestle it off his finger. He felt foolish for a moment. He even blushed, not that anyone but me would notice beneath the ale-flush. Then he scowled, so he looked downright unfriendly when his hand was finally free of ornament and he could safely offer it to be shaken.

If somebody had held up a mirror on front of me at that moment, I would immediately have realized I had nothing to offer Ray. Ray had no possible need of this blob. But luckily I was looking at Ted, and the part of me that was doomed to make unflattering comparisons, that was already holding everything and everybody up to this amazing Ray and finding them wanting, had something else to work on. I decided that Ted's hair was greasy, and sideboards made his face look fat. Everyone wore sideboards in those days, even me, even Ray, though his were neat, and the strong symmetry of his face would have been able to ride out the fashions of any decade.

I noticed that even Ted's leathers looked sorry for themselves, scuffed and faded, while Ray's looked as if they'd just been oiled. Not new or anything, just beautifully broken in and cared for.

I knew perfectly well that Ted wanted a private word with me about the change of plan. He kept jerking his head, to mean I should come aside for a while, but when I didn't budge it made him look as if there was something wrong with his neck. Nerves. I wasn't nervy at all. It felt wonderful just standing next to Ray, standing doing nothing, and watching the way the world changed round him.

Finally Ted had exhausted his options, and he asked me: "Are you sure you know what you're doing?" To which the honest answer could only be No. It was because I didn't know what I was doing that I needed to go along with Ray, wherever it was that he was going. And of course I said Yes.

Thinking about it, Ted's part in all this was pretty small. He didn't need to look so solemn. All he had to do was make a phone call. He didn't even need to speak to my Dad direct, he was only passing a message along. Strange to think that as late as 1975 my parents didn't have the phone. Marjorie next door would take the message, and it was Marjorie who would trot across to tell my Dad I wasn't coming home. Marjorie was still mobile in 1975, still sighted and able to get around. In 1975 there were still a few people called Marjorie. A few Ediths, a few Ivys.

Ted was in the clear. Ted could drink as late as he liked. I'd worn Ted's spare helmet on the way to Box Hill, and now he swung it rather sullenly towards me. He almost threw it. Perhaps he was offended by Ray's keeping his gloves on when they shook hands, or the whole kerfuffle of the business with the ring pull, the ring pull he'd thrown to the ground like a man in a silly strop breaking off an engagement.

The helmet I was to wear had a shabby, secondhand look. Almost a junk-shop look. It was easy to believe that it had fallen off a barstool more than once, just like the man who was lending it to me. I hoped I'd never find out how much or how little protection it had to offer, after so many tavern impacts. Even before I needed to put it on I could tell that it smelled of beer. Perhaps he drank out of it, for a bet, or not needing even that much of an excuse. Perhaps that was his secret sense of himself, as a sort of Viking. Ted the biking Viking.

Ray said nothing while we walked the few hundred yards to where he'd left his bike. I can't think of a word to describe the way he walked: "stroll" is all wrong, unless you add in a huge assurance, an authority that radiated from him with every casual step. Kings don't stroll. I could feel myself scurrying after him on legs that seemed stumpier than ever before, anxious to keep up but dreading the inevitable moment when he would turn to me and say, "You didn't really think you were coming home with me, did you? Try looking in a mirror sometime, when you're feeling strong." That had to be his game, his way of getting kicks. Building up my dreams to send them crashing down. But I knew that whatever happened I wasn't going to go back to Ted and to Isleworth with my tail between my legs. I'd sleep on Box Hill if I had to. Curl up in a bush.

Ray had left his helmet hanging from a handlebar of his machine. We all of us had less reason to expect our possessions to be pinched in those days, but even then I found Ray's confidence that nothing of his would be taken or tampered with extraordinary. It was as if he could fill things with a protective charge, and needn't worry that anything would happen to them while he was away.

For the first time I had a mystifying glimpse of Ray's glove ritual: the thin ones peeled off and tucked carefully in the pocket of the jacket he was carrying, the thicker gloves—gauntlets, almost—retrieved from the helmet where he had so trustingly or defiantly left them. His helmet, quite unlike mine (Ted's), gleamed softly and held no dents.

I didn't know much about bikes then, and I don't know much more now, but even at first glance Ray's machine, a black Norton Commando, put the Japanese bike on which I'd arrived at Box Hill to shame. Which was strange, since Ted's Yamaha, his pride and joy, was only a couple of months old, in the earliest stages of neglect, while the Norton was far from new. But there was a symmetry between the man and what he rode, between both men and what they rode. Ray's bike was as classic as he was—they were versions of the same superlative, he in confidence and leather, the Norton in power and chrome.

If you're a glasses-wearer, putting on a crash helmet presents quite a problem, particularly if it's full-face. If you wear glasses with wire stems, the sort that wind around your ears, I don't see how it's even possible. Even with my rigid stems I had to remember to take the glasses off—I laid them on the grass for a moment—before putting the helmet on, and only then to push the earpieces awkwardly into place.

Before I took my glasses off I had time to notice that the interior of Ted's spare helmet, which it had once seemed such a privilege to wear, the fiberglass shell of it, was matted with hairs, some mid-length and brown, which might have been anybody's, which might have been mine from the ride down, and some long and blonde, with a flip at the end, which might have been Joyce's. All girls' hair had that flip. Girls' hair in those days had learned lessons from the Partridge Family, from Abba, from Suzi Quatro. "Charlie's Angels" were just around the corner, preparing to undertake their first missions.

While I fiddled with the chinstrap Ray walked round the bike. It puzzled me that he kicked at the tires and leaned over with a frown to inspect the brakes. Over time I learned that he did these checks every time he returned to the bike after a lapse of more than a few minutes. He was always scrupulous about safety, in a way that was far from common at the time.

Back then, though, I didn't understand that what Ray was doing was admirably safety-conscious. In my uncertain state I worried that he had particular reasons for fearing a punctured tire or disabled brakes. For the first time it struck me that he might be special *in the world*, not just special to me, special because I'd never met anyone remotely like him. I wondered if he was someone famous I hadn't recognized, someone who was at risk of sabotage if he mixed with ordinary people. Ordinary people at a bikers' meeting place near Leatherhead on a Bank Holiday Monday.

I must have looked pitiful to him when he finished with his checks and turned round. I'd struggled into my jacket again, and I finally had the helmet on. I was hearing my own breathing even with the visor up, sweating so that my glasses started to fog, and I was afraid beer was condensing in my squashed hair. I was numbly convinced that he would choose the most painful possible moment to say that he'd changed his mind, and that I'd have to struggle in humiliation with the strap all over again. Instead he handed his own jacket to me, saying I might be warm now, but I'd need it later on.

Perhaps he was embarrassed by the naffness of my attempt at a leather jacket—*naff* was a word then in its prime. Princess Anne must take a lot of the credit for popularizing it, at least as a verb. She used it as a swear word that didn't offend reporters too much if they overheard it. "Naff off," she'd tell them. A disappointing horse at a gymkhana might be naffing hopeless. It was like the posh tea that the Queen drinks, the tea with the Royal Warrant. By appointment. Princess Anne gave "naff off" and "naffing" the Royal Warrant.

I saw for the first time how truly naff my jacket was. The hide was like animal cardboard, not like skin at all. And perhaps Ray was ashamed of me and wanted to cover up my mistake, but that doesn't really ring true. He couldn't be dragged down by other people's choices, however poor they were. It didn't work that way. Ray had image and to spare. The tendency was all in the other direction—for him to pull other people up, somehow.

Ray hadn't been wearing the jacket he handed me, just using it as a pillow, so it didn't smell intensely of him. I pulled it on with a sort of reverence all the same, not minding that it was much too long and wouldn't close properly round my tummy. The weight of the thing was astounding. I felt as if I was wearing an old-fashioned diving suit, the sort in the Tintin books.

Ray helped me to turn back the sleeves so that my hands struggled back into the light again, but he accepted the inevitable when it came to the zip. It wasn't going to close. His breath was minty. He met my eyes and said again, "What am I going to do with you?" This time, though, there wasn't a flicker of uncertainty in his voice. It sounded as if knew perfectly well what he was going to do. He said it in the way that people say, "Have I got news for you." Not really a question.

I was tempted to make a run for it then, before I disappointed him the way I knew I was bound to do. Of course he'd come after me and grab the jacket back, but maybe I'd be able to sneak the dress gloves out of its pocket, the gloves with the warmth still lingering from his fingers. The ones he was wearing when he let me try to please him.

He started the bike, springing up and bearing smoothly down on its kick-start in a single economical motion. You could hardly even call it a kick. The engine roared into throaty life. If everyone could kick-start a bike as smoothly as Ray, electric start would never have caught on.

I couldn't believe how noisy the Norton was. It wasn't yet dark, not by a long way, it was only late afternoon, but he turned the headlight on. He must have been one of the first people to do that, to ride with his beam on night and day. Of course not every machine back then had electrics powerful enough to sustain a permanent beam. The Norton did. His helmet was open-faced, unlike mine, and I could see the set of his mouth as well as his eyes when he nodded me to get on behind him.

Short legs aren't well suited to being slung over high objects, but I managed to lever myself into the saddle eventually. As I tried to get comfortable, I saw my knees for the first time since I'd met Ray. Of course the trousers were bagged and deeply marked with grass stains, and I understood why Ted hadn't been able to take his eyes off me long enough to notice Ray's unorthodox zip. My knees had already given him the gist of the story.

There were more adjustments to be made to the bike. With my weight on it the mirrors were misaligned, and Ray spent a few seconds while the engine warmed up setting them properly for the new load. The new load being me. Even so the bike vibrated so much that the mirrors trembled, and the information they passed to Ray must have shimmered.

I'd only traveled a few dozen miles on motorcycles in my life, and I found it hard to relax the way a good pillion should. Ray's height meant I couldn't see the road over his shoulders. He kept on turning his head round, which I found disconcerting, particularly as thanks to my full-face helmet I prodded his back with my chin every time he braked. Crazily, I kept thinking, every time he turned round, that he must just have noticed me stowing away on his bike where I so obviously didn't belong, and would pull over to push me off. If he even bothered to stop.

Later I learned that he practiced the Police Motorcycle Method of riding, and these were his "observations." He was no boy racer, no kind of speed merchant. He really cared about safety. Once again he was ahead of his time. In those days the motorcycle riding test was pretty rudimentary, from what people told me, a very basic assessment of skills. I mean, Ted passed first time, didn't he? That's evidence enough. A chap would come out of the test office, ask you to ride round the block a few times, then lunge at you for you to do your emergency stop. If you were still upright and you hadn't run over him, then you had passed. There was none of the modern stuff, an examiner following you on his own machine, giving instructions to you through a headset that links your helmets.

I'm not convinced that Ray would have talked, even if there had been a radio connecting us. At one point he shouted to me that I should hold onto him, instead of trying to grip the back of the saddle. I must have been dragging on the bike every time he accelerated. I'm bulky. I can't help it. I'm bulky. I wouldn't have dared to hold onto him unless he'd told me to.

The roughness of the ride, despite Ray's scrupulous handling, unsettled my stomach and made me burp up memories of the hamburger and glass of lemonade I'd had before I'd even known there was a Ray. I also burped up taste-memories of him, the taste of Ray's body in the only place I'd touched it. As if I was proving to myself what I'd thought when I first set eyes on him. Ray was tasty.

For a while, as we headed north from Box Hill, I thought he was taking me home to Isleworth after all, past Chessington and Surbiton, on the A243. Chessington was only a zoo in those days, it wasn't a World of Wonders. I even wondered if the whole afternoon was some sort of outlandish birthday present. But who knew me well enough to lay on a combination bike-taxi and charismatic male prostitute package? Particularly if I didn't know those were things I might want myself.

It was as if Ray clicking his fingers up by that tree earlier on—an hour ago, maybe two—had paralyzed my will. Perhaps he was a hypnotist. Perhaps that was what he did for a living. That was how he could just click his fingers and shut down some pathways in the brain, open a whole new lot up. Still, you can only be hypnotized if you let it happen. It can't be done against your will. Anyway now, as I held on to him on the back of his bike, and not just because he told me to, part of me was like someone on stage at the end of a hypnotist's show.

After the man with the eyes that look right through you clicks his fingers the second time, the people on stage wake up and realize that what they've been champing on with such relish is actually an onion and not an apple. The sweetness and the vileness fighting each other for a moment in the mouth and in the memory, before the sweetness goes for good.

Bits of my mind started to come alive again, and to connect up with other bits. One bit was still shouting to itself in horrified triumph, *I sucked a man's cock—real-life blow job—I sucked a cock and didn't throw up!* And another part of me was thinking that I didn't have the first idea of where this stranger was taking me, or what would happen to me when I got there.

When we crossed the river at Kingston Ray turned left instead of carrying straight on to Isleworth. The air was cool and moist by the river. Even double-jacketed, I wasn't any too warm and Ray must have been freezing, but he gave no sign.

Ray turned right after a couple of miles. It turned out he

lived in Hampton, in a cul-de-sac off the High Street. The cul-de-sac was called Cardinals Paddock. No need to guess which cardinal—there's not much inside a five-mile radius of Hampton Court that doesn't trade on old Wolsey. As I climbed off the bike, stumbling on gravel, I could see a stretch of old wall with flowerbeds against it. For all I know, it *was* Cardinal Wolsey's paddock, or what was left of it after five hundred years or so.

Like a fool I undid the strap without thinking, and pulled the helmet off without removing my glasses, so I mangled the stems a bit. I had to hold the specs against my head with one hand to stop them falling off. I felt even clumsier than usual, with the helmet in the other hand.

Ray held the front door for me and bounced up the stairs two at a time to his flat. I did my best to follow him, but I've always had one leg stronger than the other, so all I could do was two stairs then one, two then one. I was out of breath by the time I had reached the first floor, and my glasses were misted again now, as well as wonky. I put the helmet down.

When we were both inside he raised his hands to me, and I flinched back from him. Ted's Viking helmet banged against the wall. I almost dropped it. I didn't dare look down in case it had left a scuff mark on the wall, a stripe of beer and human hair.

Only that morning my gentle Dad had raised his hand to me, and it looked as if my birthday was going to be the day everyone got their blows in. Dad had slapped me, because of something I'd told him about my visit to the hospital with Joyce the day before. The ward sister had asked us to leave because we were making Mum laugh, and Dad got terribly angry when I told him about it. I just didn't understand. *I'd* have been worried about Mum if we hadn't been able to make her laugh. We didn't say people "overreacted" then, or else this would have been a classic case of a person overreacting. Me trying to cheer him up and Dad flying off the handle.

When Ray came towards me a second time with his hands raised, I'd already realized he wasn't really going to strangle me. I was even able to think, Just my luck, he's going to strangle me without going to the trouble of raping me first, which shows that I wasn't really worried. Of course he was only grasping the lapels of his heavy jacket to peel it off me. Then he hung it carefully on a peg. There were leather jackets on the pegs next to it, so that I thought, How many people live here? It didn't occur to me that anyone could own more than one leather jacket. When I took off my own naff leather jacket, he didn't offer it the hospitality of a peg, and I didn't blame him for that. It didn't deserve any better than to lie on the floor.

When I flinched from Ray my glasses almost fell off my face, so he noticed there was a problem with them. He took them off to another room to do something about it. I stayed where I was, thinking that was safest. I could hear the clatter of a household drawer being opened, a gloved hand rummaging softly among tools.

I was stranded without my glasses, I needed a pee and I was starting to get hungry, and of course the moment Ray was out of the room I knew quite clearly that he meant me no good and that I had been mad to go with him. Nobody knew where I was.

In two minds. It's a usual phrase, but it's a rotten feeling when you spend half the time thinking one thing—I'm safe, this is fine—and then you switch to panic certainty, you're done for and it's all your fault. It was exhausting not being able to settle to one way of thinking.

Then Ray came back and fitted the repaired specs back on

my face. He'd done something clever with pliers. He seemed perfectly calm. It stood to reason that if he was planning to do me harm he'd be more excited. He'd taken the bike gloves off to do the repair, and I tried not to look at his hands. I'd decided he must have birthmarks or scars on them, to keep them covered up so much of the time, but they were perfect strong pianist's hands. Not that I know any pianists, it's just something people say about fingers they like. Ray caught me looking and smiled at me with a bit of mockery, as if he knew what I'd been thinking. He even turned them over slowly in front of me, so I could get a good look from every angle. Ray's smile was beautiful, but it made me uneasy. I couldn't see what I had done to deserve it.

He asked me if there was anything I needed, and I managed to blurt out about needing a piss and something to eat. Something to nibble anyway. And Ray said: "Why don't I show you where everything is, and you can look after yourself?"

It seems absurd now how few times I'd seen the inside of people's houses up to that point—mainly my parents' friends, and a few of Joyce's. My older sister, Donna, she was older enough that she didn't want her kid brother hanging around, and anyway she'd always been the type that wants to leave home as soon as she can and get stuck in to her own life.

I'd certainly never been inside a modern flat decorated in a modern way. I'd never seen windows that went down to the ground, for a start, so that the wall was mainly glass. I'd never seen spotlights in a private home, and Ray had spotlights in every room, including the bathroom. The lounge was dominated by an enormous black leather sofa with chrome armrests. It hardly seemed like a sofa at all, being so angular, or not my idea of a sofa: nothing round or bulgy about it. I knew people with record collections, I even called the few LPs I had myself "my record collection," but I'd never seen a room with a whole wall of shelving which held as many records as books. Ray had a big reel-to-reel tape recorder, as well as a professional-looking record player with a perspex top, and a separate shelf of tapes in gray plastic cases.

I didn't know it at the time, but Ray often used music to set the scene. On this occasion, though, he didn't put anything on either deck, but I don't think he had forgotten. He was just setting the scene with silence instead. Letting the silence build.

He fetched a can of beer from a fridge twice the size of the one at home, and settled himself on the sofa. There wasn't much in the fridge besides beer, some milk and a sliced loaf. With anyone but Ray, I'd have thought it was a bit poncy, having a fridge so much bigger than you need.

When you switched on the lights in the bathroom, a fan came on with a whir, which gave me a bit of a start. Ray had a shower head fixed to the wall above the bath, and a glass panel to intercept splashes. The shower at Mum and Dad's fitted over the bath taps, not very reliably.

After I'd had my pee, I had a good look at myself in the mirror. Blue eyes are supposed to be an advantage, but I don't see how they can be when they're a mucky blue like mine. Blue eyes should be a strong color like Ray's. My eyes wobble the whole time when I look at myself in a mirror. I can't seem to fix them so they're still. I wonder if they're like that all the time, wobbly rabbit eyes, or if it's just me in the mirror that sets them off.

After my pee I went into the kitchen and wolfed down some of the bread from the fridge. I could see a big steel toaster but I didn't want to keep Ray waiting, and I wasn't sure how to work it. There wasn't any butter but I found some jam. Then I put the kettle on. I'd not come across an electric kettle before—I knew they existed, obviously, I didn't live in a time warp, I'd watched *Tomorrow's World* since I was eight or something, but my parents used the hob. Ray's kitchen was all-electric, though, and the kettle looked more like a metal jug plugged into the wall. I filled it and pressed the switch so a light came on. To be fair to myself, that jug style wasn't common for a long time after. Maybe it was a prototype or something imported.

I couldn't keep still, and though I was trying to play it cool, I kept looking in on Ray in the lounge. I noticed he had put the dress gloves on—I thought then that he had retrieved them from his jacket while I had my pee, which he may have done, but I didn't even consider the possibility that he had more than one pair. More than likely it was another pair.

He didn't speak to me, or look at me directly. I kept shuffling from watching the kettle in the kitchen to hovering over Ray, and he was kind enough not to make me feel stupid by pointing out that I didn't need to watch the kettle, which would turn itself off without my help when it had boiled. Of course I only thought of that later on. I can't believe how patient he was. He absolutely didn't rush me.

When he had finished his beer he shook the can significantly and raised his eyebrow. I didn't need subtitles to know he wanted me to fetch another, and I wasn't offended that he didn't say thank you when I brought it. When I came in at last with my cup of tea, I must admit that I was a bit put out that he stretched out his gloved hand to bar me from the place on the sofa next to him. I suppose I was being a bit sneaky making myself at home, but he'd told me to help myself from the fridge so I didn't realize I was taking a liberty in the lounge.

When he stretched out his hand, I thought he meant I should

sit on the end furthest from him, but when I made my way over there he just shook his head—still without meeting my eyes. The leather of his one-piece suit accompanied his gestures with a supple creaking.

In a way it was insulting that he warned me off the sofa as if I was a dog that would leave stray hairs on it. But if he hadn't given me any guidance, how would I have ended up where I wanted to be but would never dare to suggest, curled up at his feet? He didn't tell me what to do. He didn't say that I had no right to a chair, any more than my naff jacket had a right to a peg. In a strange way he freed my choices, though he seemed to take them away. There was a matching armchair opposite the sofa, and I could perfectly well have gone over to that. Of course I'll never know whether he would actually have let me sit there, but knowing his nature better now, I think he would have. He just wasn't interested in forcing people.

After all the palaver of making the tea I didn't get the chance to drink it. Ray simply moved it out of my reach. Obviously he had realized that I needed something to do with my hands, and that if he just let me get rid of my fidgets I wouldn't disappoint him. Ray was good at waiting. Even his waiting wasn't like ordinary people's waiting. His waiting was decisive. He decided that I had needed to make that cup of tea, but I didn't need to drink it.

Ray took my glasses off for me. If I'd been told before it happened that I would be blindfolded the night I lost my virginity, I would have had one of my panics. But when Ray took a black handkerchief, folded it slowly and then knotted it round my head to blot out my vision, I was almost relieved. The thing I'd never been able to imagine about sex, as it might apply to me, was how anyone would ever have the patience to show me what to do. I couldn't see it happening, not to me. Now as Ray deftly knotted the black hankie behind my head, I knew it was under way at last. It no longer mattered that I didn't have the first clue. Someone else was taking responsibility.

When he started to take my clothes off, I minded a lot less than I would have without the hankie. He undressed me not roughly and not gently, just efficiently. I found I could cope with Ray seeing my body, as long as I didn't have to see it myself.

Ray pulled me up to my knees facing him. Obviously he had decided that I needed something stronger than tea. It may not have occurred to him that I wasn't any sort of drinker. On special occasions Dad would pour me a glass of "shandy," which was really only lemonade with a splash of beer in it. He made a big show of it, as if two sips would have me roaring, and I suppose I believed I was being allowed into the world of the grown-ups. Mum and Dad drank advocaat on special occasions, and from the time I was twelve they let me have some at Christmas—only it was really only custard, in a little glass like the ones they were using. Since I was sixteen they'd given me actual advocaat, but I actually preferred the custard, and I would have asked to go back to the old routine if I hadn't been afraid of seeming a baby.

Suddenly there was warmth against my mouth, and roughness and cold and wet. I opened my lips and Ray let beer trickle from his mouth to mine. I coughed and choked on the sour-tasting liquid. If I had been a beer-breathing creature from some sort of lager planet he would have been giving me the kiss of life, but I was only dazed Colin from Isleworth and I couldn't cope. Then when I'd choked on the taste I realized there was another taste behind it, the elusive taste of Ray's tongue. I wanted that. The tastiness of him inside his mouth.

Still, my fear of drink was stronger than my curiosity about kissing, and it paralyzed me. Ray took another gulp of beer, but this time I kept my mouth shut against him, until he used his tongue as a slippery crowbar to overcome my defenses. His tongue turned to a warm liquid inside the cold stream of the beer as it entered my mouth. It vanished before I could find it with mine.

This was very clearly not a kiss, but it also wasn't the opposite of a kiss. I found if I opened my mouth obediently for each new gulp Ray kept his tongue well back, and I didn't dare to do any exploring of my own. But if I resisted a little, his tongue would play against my mouth until I gave in. Once or twice I was able to taste his tongue, and feel again its warmth through the coldness of the beer.

Watching kissing done in films, I'd always been puzzled that people seemed to close their eyes the moment anything happened. Wasn't the whole point of the exercise that you could gaze into your lover's eyes? Now, blindfolded in the middle of my first real drink, something I didn't want, and the near-kiss I wanted more than anything, I realized that gazing didn't come into it.

After ten minutes of this I was fainting with pleasure and frustration, and also fairly sloshed. Ray left at one point, it must have been to get another can of beer, and already I was unsure of my whereabouts in space—where the door and windows of the room were. Ray was trying to orient me by touch and taste, in the world of my less developed senses. He was also making me relax, whether I wanted to or not. Obviously I can't tell how much of the beer went down his throat instead of mine, but I think he only drank enough to keep me company.

There was a time when the small ads in gay papers were very indirect in their suggestions—very circumspect. Now of course you can say absolutely bloody anything. But in between, when you could say so much and no more, there was a time when people referred to O-levels and A-levels. Of course they meant Oral and Anal, but when I first saw those ads I honestly thought they were talking about qualifications. It's a sore point with me. I left school at fifteen, and I've got O-levels, and I know I'm not stupid. But it's not difficult to make me feel as if I am. I didn't leave school because I'd learned all I wanted to know. I left school because I was short and fat and tired of being bullied.

I'm passionate about education. It's really important to me, and it's not something I ever take for granted. When I have a class, my workmates help me out by organizing their shifts to fit in. They're very good about it. They tease me a bit about using long words and always taking a book with me into the cab, but I don't mind that. My job nickname is Brainiac. It's fine being teased by people who know you and like you, it's almost the opposite of the other kind of teasing, the deadly kind you get at school.

Anyway, Ray got me to revise my O-levels for a few minutes, and then he decided it was time for my sexual education to get advanced. He pulled me to my feet and half-dragged, half-lifted me across to the bed. If he'd told me where we were going, I could have made the short trip less awkwardly, but I suppose he wanted me a bit confused, to make me stumble as he used his strength to get me where I was meant to be.

From the moment he shut the door of his flat behind us Ray hadn't been communicating with me, in the way that people normally communicate. Small talk, big talk, talk that's in between. He had hardly said a word. You could say, though, that he was teaching me a different, specialized way of communicating. Until now he had been gentle enough, without being exactly considerate. But now there was a change. There was none of the patience he had showed when he was using my mouth.

He chucked me down on the bed. The body I had experienced as decisiveness and strength I now suffered as sheer weight and invasion. He pinned me down. And what had begun as a rough seduction ended as, well, rape. I'd said he could do anything with me. I know that. But some things can't be consented to. Drunk or sober, no one could agree to being opened up so fiercely. If he used any lubricant at all he was sparing with it, but I don't think he did. I wasn't even entitled to a smear of the candle grease that his leathers benefited from. He didn't let me adjust to the insult of his cock, or the rhythm of its hurting.

At some stage I found there was a belt in my mouth. Ray didn't mean it as a gag—if he'd wanted to silence me he was well able to do it. I bit down on the belt, but it didn't exactly keep me quiet. Belt or no belt, I made a lot of noise. The next time I saw the dentist, it turned out I'd chipped a tooth, but that could have happened in a number of ways. Eating a peach and crunching the stone by mistake. Gnawing too greedily on the bones when Mum cooked lamb chops.

At least he was quick—and I don't think he was doing it for pleasure. He made me suffer, but he didn't feed on my suffering. The way he had been earlier on was much more in character, implacable but not cruel. It's just that I think this was a special occasion for him. For both of us.

Of course there's an unromantic part of me that still can't accept how different he was when he was teaching me to suck cock, and it's a part that whispers in my ear: *If you had a set of teeth up your arse, he'd be gentle there too.* But I think it was a sort of ceremony for him. He wasn't doing it for fun, exactly. There was a reason. He was taking possession.

I'd thought he was going to kill me with his cock, but when I found he hadn't, after a while I started to cheer up, and to think it hadn't been too bad, all in all. I'd never looked forward to being fucked, not ever. I'd thought it was all going to be much worse.

Meanwhile Ray had other things in store for me. Before I was allowed to sleep I lost some virginities I didn't even know I had. He had me doing things I'd never thought of doing, so I'd never thought of myself as someone who hadn't done them. I licked a boot for the first time, I licked a man's arse. I was far too surprised to feel any shame. It had never occurred to me that doing these things could be made to mean something.

One thing I really appreciated about Ray's way of doing things, that night and afterwards, was that he didn't touch my cock or expect me to play with it. I was glad of that. I'm not a big boy down there, and there's another thing, which is that my stiffies don't turn up on any particular schedule. They show up when they want to, usually when there's no one around. If I'm shy as a whole person, then my cock is the shyest part of me by far, as well as the part of me that I'm shyest about. It was a relief that Ray treated my cock pretty much as if it didn't exist.

It sounds incredible, and maybe my memory isn't up to scratch, but I seem to remember that Ray fucked me again before we slept. The second time may not have come so soon, I don't see how it could have, but whenever it happened, he took his time and I enjoyed it. The pain had a rhythm and the rhythm was pleasure. Ray never hurt me again. The hurting and the kissing were both over by the end of that first night.

When Ray had gone to sleep, it was already getting light and birds were singing. I could see the belt I'd bitten and the hankie that had covered my eyes on the pillow between us. Ray had black sheets and pillowcases, another thing I'd never seen. If I rolled the sheet down a bit I could also sneak a look at his midsection and compare it to mine. It was hard to believe that they were equivalent parts of similar creatures, from a strict anatomical point of view. The flat curve of his belly. I could even stroke it, softly. The beauty of his breathing and being alive. I could lull myself to sleep by counting the number of sit-ups that would work the miracle and turn my tummy into his, counting down from a billion.

Ray's willpower broke over me three times in twenty-four hours, in waves that overtook each other to spill relentlessly forward. At Box Hill he had taken the initiative, turning my stumble over his leg into the first step on a new path. Then he chose me to spend the night with him, he who could have had anyone. He who could have had anyone. And now when I woke up in Cardinals Paddock on Bank Holiday, horribly sore but in my own way also horribly proud, proud even of the being sore, he had made more plans. He never told me his plans, but then he never told anyone his plans. His plans weren't secret, they were only private.

He'd made coffee and showered; now it was my turn. If I wanted to, I could imagine him looking at me while I slept, the same way I'd watched over him the night before. Except that when I tried to think of that, I could only imagine him shaking his head all over again, the way he had at Box Hill. Wondering if he should take a long walk and hope I'd do the decent thing, let myself out and make myself scarce.

Ray had tidied away the belt and the hankie, the beer cans and the cup of tea I never got to drink. He waited until I'd drunk my coffee and taken my shower, and then he said he'd give me a ride home.

I really wasn't looking forward to confronting Dad. Mum being in hospital, his mind wasn't really on me or he would never have lost his temper on my birthday morning, or if he did he would just have shouted at me and left it at that. Not that he was much of a shouter. I think we were both shocked that he had raised his hand to me, but I wasn't going to pretend it hadn't happened.

Mum and Dad were a textbook perfect couple, except that people are always a little shocked by that sort of closeness in real life. They always saw eye to eye—that's what we said, which was partly a joke because they were exactly the same height. They weren't lovey-dovey, exactly, though they still held hands a lot, breaking off if people were watching. If the person watching was Joyce or me, they'd give each other a last squeeze, but still they'd stop holding hands. They weren't broadcasting the success of their marriage, they just lived inside it.

There's a village with a quaint custom—there's a prize of a side of bacon given every year to a married couple who haven't had a single quarrel. It's called the Dunmow flitch. Mum and Dad could have won that bacon year after year. They'd have got sick of bacon. They had every possible qualification. Well, apart from not living in Great Dunmow.

They worked together, Dad being the pharmacist and Mum running the shop side of things. Before they had kids they lived over the shop, and then they moved, but only down the street, five doors away from the chemist's.

I don't think Joyce and I ever thought Mum and Dad got married to have us. They got married to have each other. When I say "Joyce and I," I don't include Donna because it's not the sort of conversation I can imagine having with her, that's all. I'm sure that Donna and Joyce and I were planned—we weren't accidental. But the marriage was the master plan. It took us a while to realize that other people's parents weren't like ours. Their anniversary was a big day for them, and they didn't share it. On that day every year we would stay overnight with neighbors, even if Mum and Dad weren't going away. So it made sense that Mum being in hospital was going to turn Dad inside out.

I thought if I got home late enough he'd be at the hospital, and when he got back I'd say I was just leaving to visit her, and then it would be evening by the time we had no alternative but to deal with each other. I tried to delay the moment that Ray and I set off on the bike from Hampton, but Ray wouldn't take no for an answer. As I was beginning to understand, not taking no for an answer was pretty much his life's work.

Dad was just leaving. He was actually opening the door on his way out as I came up the path with the key in my hand. Dad looked blank for a moment, but he had the good grace to invite Ray in. Then the impulse to be hospitable stalled just inside the door. In this awful week for him, Dad's social graces fell short of the front room, so that we just stood there awkwardly in the little hall.

I suppose most dads would flinch if a six-and-a-half-foot biker came striding up their path, but that side of things didn't seem to register with mine. Both my sisters had gone out with plenty of bikers, Donna had married one the year before and Joyce would tie the knot with the one she chose over Ted in 1976. Bikers are in our blood.

Those were different times. Motorcycles were still poor man's transport. They weren't a big statement. Insurance hadn't gone silly yet. Young men rode bikes till they married.

Sometimes the bike lasted until there was a pram. Sometimes the bike and pram stared each other down for a few months, though the pram always won in the end.

Plus Ray was an older man, but he wasn't an *older* older man. He was what you would make up if you wanted an imaginary older brother for your only son. As best as I can work it out, he was in his late twenties.

In my parents' hallway Ray did the talking. He said: "Mr. Smith, I've asked Colin to stay with me in Hampton for a few days. I think he needs a bit of room. Maybe you both do." Which stunned me. I didn't remember saying anything to Ray about what was happening at home. Who knows? Maybe I talk in my sleep, only there isn't usually somebody there to listen.

Dad took it in his stride. It helped that Ray was well-spoken, without being snobby-posh. Back then every voice on the radio sounded a bit toffy, a bit far-back, even if they were people from all over who'd taken lessons to sound the same as each other. Most people still preferred the cultured voices on the radio to the sounds they made themselves.

Dad was even relieved not to have to deal with me. In his mind, he was already at the hospital, he was already with Mum. And because of what Ray had said, we could both go to the hospital together, and not need to thrash things out. The pressure was off, suddenly. Ray said he'd pick me up at six—me and my toilet bag.

So Dad's mind wasn't fully on me, which was a little bit painful, but if I'm honest the same went double the other way round. My mind wasn't on Dad. Ray stood by the Norton as we pulled away in Dad's car, and I couldn't take my eyes off him. He didn't wave, he didn't smile. He didn't do anything to make me worry he'd not turn up at the time he'd said.

If I'd been paying more attention to my little Dad, I might have noticed how Mum's illness was affecting him. I was too amazed by the changes in my own life to see that something fairly drastic was happening to him.

Pharmacist or no pharmacist, Dad was inhibited about illness in women and women's conditions, and the fact that Mum had just gone through what his generation called the change of life made him even more tight-lipped. I only learned what was the matter with Mum from Joyce, who had female grapevine privileges. The matter with Mum was cervical polyps, which were very likely to be benign—it was a hundred to one they meant her no harm—but they were taking no chances and running plenty of tests. Joyce wasn't worried, she told me Mum wasn't worried, so I didn't worry, but either Dad was getting something to worry about from someone else or he was getting the whole thing out of proportion.

His hair went white, not overnight, but over a fortnight—fifteen days to be exact—and this must have been a few days into the change. There was almost as much salt as pepper in his hair at this point, and in another ten days there would only be salt. No dark grains at all.

Ray arrived at six, as he'd said he would, and I had my toilet bag ready. That day I moved in with Ray, the day after I'd met him. How's that for changing your life in a hurry? But at the same time I never exactly moved out of Mum and Dad's. I had two addresses, two very different ways of life, though the distance between them on the map was only small—five miles, if that. I didn't become two people, but I suppose I did become a person whose life had two different sides to it.

Of course at first I had a horribly strong feeling of being in Hampton on a trial basis. I thought I was on approval, and would be boxed up and sent back where I came from if I didn't come up to scratch, though Ray never said anything to give that impression. I came up with that idea all by myself. It's the sort of idea my mind spins out all the time.

I tried to work out what my place in the household was, apart from the obvious. What do you do for the man who is everything? I tried to tidy up, until he told me not to, to leave everything as it was. Then I decided that the cooking must be my department, and he didn't tell me any different, so I set myself to that. I struggled to put meals together, undecided between the plain and the fancy, fish fingers one day, my forlorn attempt at coq au vin the next, while Ray ate without comment, day after day. He cleaned his plate, but without passing judgment. I'd look up to him, trying not to read too much into his expression. It took me ages to relax.

Maybe any two people, every two people, have one thing in common, one thing at the least, and I took my time to realize that this was where Ray was like my little Dad. He really didn't care what he ate. He ate what was put in front of him. If there was a second similarity between that particular pair, though, I never found it.

Apart from my difficulties in understanding how I fitted into it, Ray's domestic life was entirely regular and orderly. On Saturday mornings he cleaned the bike; Saturday night was always poker night. The game convened in the members' houses by rotation, so every six weeks or so Ray played host. He took me with him on club nights from the first, but I never got interested in the game—either the technicalities or its underlying psychology. It wasn't a problem. Nobody minded if I brought along a book and read it quietly.

Sundays there was always a bike run. The membership of

Ray's bike club was exactly the same as the membership of his poker club. You couldn't ride with the bike club unless you played poker, and you couldn't play poker unless you rode with the bike club. It was all the same fellows—Big Steve and Little Steve, Mark, Paul, Alan and the others. It's just that for Saturday night and the poker game, bike riding wasn't compulsory, the way it would have been for an actual bike club meeting.

Alan was the odd man out. The others liked to act mean, but he sometimes seemed like the real thing, which isn't so attractive. He didn't wash. You could imagine him sleeping in his leathers—in fact, you couldn't imagine anything else. There was a shine on all the others, on Ray, obviously, but also on the others. There was no shine on Alan.

Ray may not have made the rules, but he seemed to be the one to enforce them. He was strict about drinking. Members could have one drink on a Saturday evening, and no more, if they were biking—so there was the loophole, if people really wanted to drink, that they didn't have to bring their machines on a Saturday night.

Ray himself always rode to the bike club meetings, and never even had the single drink his rules allowed. Only when he was the host at poker night, every couple of months, at home in Hampton, did he have a few carefully spaced tumblers of Scotch. I never saw him drunk.

Bets on poker night tended to be modest. Maybe that was because some members were comfortably off, and some weren't. The biker lifestyle made people's differences less glaring, but it couldn't be expected to make them disappear. There was no set maximum bet, but members were expected to donate half of their winnings to the expense of food and drink. Any actual surplus subsidized the bike runs.

The club made regular expeditions to Box Hill, but also to destinations further out, like Bath and Bristol, preferring to head west rather than cross London. The members came from Teddington and West Byfleet and Woking, from different walks of life, so that sometimes poker night took place in a large detached house, and sometimes we squeezed into a rather poky flat. If the weather was unusually cold and there was no central heating, Ray didn't mind if I wore a few clothes.

All the members of the club rode British bikes. BSAs, Triumphs, Nortons, Royal Enfields. There wasn't an actual rule about that, but the peer pressure would have been pretty overwhelming. Most of them had kick-starts, though Ray was the only one who never seemed to need more than one kick, one authoritative nudge with his boot, to make the engine catch.

The domestic bike industry was already dead in 1975, but the club hadn't really noticed. There was still plenty of British iron on the roads. Nobody bought new, even if they had the money. People preferred to buy second hand, and they weren't afraid of a bit of maintenance. Spare parts weren't difficult to come by just yet.

Ray was always at the front of the motorcade, if that's the word. The stately rush of chrome in procession. He wasn't an officer of the club, but then the club had no officers. He was just a natural leader. Lads on building sites and road works would often make the vroom-vroom gesture at us as we passed, the revving of an imaginary throttle, and sometimes, just sometimes, Ray would oblige. I noticed that the bikes in the pack behind me only ever played to the crowd by revving their engines if Ray had given the lead. These days even royalty acknowledges the cheers of well-wishers, but Ray showed no interest.

Ray's safety-mindedness meant that he wanted the bike

club to spread out properly on the road, and not bunch to-gether dangerously. What he actually said was: "I don't want you berks breathing down my neck." In fact all that happened was that the other riders left Ray some space, and then they all bunched together a little distance behind him. Perhaps Ray wasn't too annoyed by this, the way the club divided on the road into a charismatic outrider and a following pack. A thor-oughbred pulling away from a field of also-rans. You couldn't argue with that. He was the only one of the bunch who read a newspaper that didn't print horoscopes.

Except that this thoroughbred was a stickler for speed limits, whether he was leading the pack or riding alone, and invariably stopped at pedestrian crossings when someone was waiting, or even approaching. Perhaps it amused him to show good man-ners when nothing was expected of him but thuggish haste. I noticed that the pedestrians he deferred to, however infirm, scuttled across the road, as if they were mortified rather than pleased that he put their lowly interests before his own. Some-how by treating them with respect he drew their attention to their own worthlessness.

I went into the bathroom soon after I moved in with Ray and couldn't find anything from my toilet bag—no cologne, no antiperspirant. I was going to ask him where he'd put my stuff when I saw them in the bathroom bin. He'd thrown my things away without saying a word to me. He'd also left the evidence of what he'd done in plain view, as if he wanted me to understand something.

I was put out, but I had enough sense to lock myself in the bathroom for a moment to think about the message Ray was sending me. He'd thrown away everything in my toilet bag that carried a fragrance. He didn't want me to smell of anything but myself, that was pretty clear. I suppose he wanted me to take pride in my body, or not to be ashamed of it at any rate. Easy for him to say: if I'd had his body, I'd have been proud of that. And he'd thrown away my aftershave but not my razor. Disposable razors were on the market, but they gave a pretty brutal shave. Razors only had the one blade. Nobody would have known what you meant if you said "shaving system." Most people in those days had safety razors that you unscrewed, though I had one of the new cartridge ones, so that the blade wasn't exposed while you changed it. Having a chemist's in the family brings some benefit.

My razor was still where I'd left it, by the basin, but my after-shave was in the bin. I stopped, trying to work out the incon-sistency. It wasn't that he wanted me to stop shaving, he just didn't like my aftershave. He wanted me not to use any cologne or antiperspirant, but he wanted me to use a *nicer* aftershave, one that he liked. So what was I supposed to do, use his?

So I started to use his, and he never said a word. And if it was a test, then I suppose I'd passed it. I wish I could say I learned to take a pride in my body. But though there was a lot I could learn from him, I couldn't learn that. There was no prospect of me imitating him there. In the short term, of course, I was more ashamed if anything—ashamed in a more complicated way that included being ashamed of being ashamed. But perhaps some of Ray's underlying message got through after all, over the months and the years. That if I was good enough for him, then unlikely as it might seem I must be good enough for me.

One Saturday morning about a month after I'd moved in, Ray went downstairs to clean the bike as usual, and I borrowed a tall stool from the kitchen and sat in the lounge window watching him do it. Cardinals Paddock was a quiet cul-de-sac, the sort of place driving schools send their cars on a Sunday afternoon to practice three-point turns, but I was always amazed at Ray's trust in the world. He never even locked the bike. Essentially it was protected by its beauty. It didn't even have a lock on the petrol tank, so all it would take would be a teenager with a match and the thought, "Why should he have that if I can't?" in his head, and Ray's great treasure would be all flame and melting.

I took up my position on the kitchen stool and watched him at work. He was very thorough—he even drew a clean cloth tenderly back and forth between the spokes of the wheels. I saw a motorcycle being flossed long before I ever knew you could do the same thing with teeth.

For the hour or so it took him to clean the bike to his standards he never once looked up. A few minutes after I'd perched on my stool it began to bother me that he didn't show any signs of noticing me—as if I was so insignificant I was invisible. But he knew I was there. Obviously he knew I was there.

It was like those Russian experiments in the paranormal we used to hear so much about. If someone predicts the cards being turned up one hundred percent of the time, then it can't be coincidence. That's proof of ESP, proof that mind reading is a reality. But if someone never guesses a card right, not ever, it can't be coincidence either. That proves ESP too, it's just not so crude a proof.

Obviously Ray knew I was there watching him the whole time, otherwise he would have had to look up at least once in a solid hour. Law of averages. So he knew I was there the whole time, and he chose not to acknowledge me. As for why he preferred the subtler way of showing we were attuned to one another, well: one-way sharing was the sort he liked best.

I can't explain it any better than that. One-way sharing was the sort he liked best.

As for why, I have no idea. It's what worked for him. And in fact, after Ray had paid me no obvious attention for a while, it seemed to me that the atmosphere below me had changed. The air gradually thickened and clotted with secret excitement. Ray's movements never speeded up or became flustered, but they were more and more loaded with sexual consequence. By the time he had polished the last square inch of elegant and potent metal, my heart was in my mouth. By now I was dreading his looking up as much as I had wanted it to happen when I started to watch. If he looked up, oh God if he *winked* at me, the whole extraordinary moment would fall to the ground and blow away.

Luckily Ray was not a man who winked, and he never looked up, never broke the spell. I stayed watching him until the bike was gleaming, but before I heard the front door open I'd returned the stool to the kitchen. Keeping my side of the bargain, so there was no visible evidence of the whole little drama played out between us, in the lounge and below the windows.

I enjoyed the weekends. I'd have Saturday lunch over at Mum and Dad's, so even if I hadn't seen them during the week, which I usually did, I kept in touch. I liked the poker club and the bike club. This was the first group I'd had anything to do with that actually seemed to work. They looked out for each other, and they shared things. They took turns choosing the music that was played on a Saturday night. Paul would choose and then Little Steve would choose and then Mark would choose, turn and turn about, an LP at a time.

Up to then the group I knew best had been my Wolf Cub troop, and I was one of those Wolf Cubs who don't go on to be

Boy Scouts, who draw a line under the experience as soon as they can. I'd try not to be noticed in the church hall, hoping no one would tease me for the fact that the buttons on my uniform kept flying off, and I still had stabilizers on my bike.

If there'd been a needlework badge I could have got that. Obviously I didn't ask if there was such a thing. But I'd taught myself to sew the buttons back on my uniform, and learned to reinforce them. I was too ashamed to ask Mum. Then when the buttons were secure the weak points became the seams, and I had to learn how to repair them and even shift them a fraction to get a little more room.

We kept on being told by Akela to Do Your Best, Do Your Best, Do Your Best, and we were forever bellowing back that we would Do Our Best, Do Our Best, Do Our Best, but no one gave me the impression that my best was worth anything. By the time I finally got my knots badge Akela had pretty much given up on me.

I know not every Cub can make Sixer, but at the end of every session after the pledge two Cubs are chosen to take down the banners ceremonially, and I was never one of them. I must have radiated incompetence and the absence of leadership skills in an organization that only existed to build them up. It doesn't really make sense, though, I don't think. If there are to be leaders then there must be followers, and I had followership skills in plenty, just waiting to be tapped.

To this day I can't see a fat kid in shorts without wanting to rush over and give what comfort I can. To tell him it won't always be like this.

So the twin clubs that made up Ray's social life were a bit of an eye-opener for me. I tried to fit my sense of how they worked into my scanty picture of the world. The sixties had only been over for five years, it had been the sixties for most of my life, and the word that came to my mind as I looked up from my book, on one of those early Saturday nights, was *commune*. This must be what a commune was. All for one. And one for all.

Weekdays were different. Ray wanted me out of the house by nine o'clock, and he didn't want me back till six. It wasn't that the routine suited me especially badly, but it certainly nipped in the bud any idea that the flat at Cardinals Paddock was my home. Home is a place you can go whenever you want. Isleworth and Mum and Dad's was home. And somehow I knew from the start that living by Ray's rules wasn't a test. Or if it was a test, it was a test that would never be over, and I'd just have to keep on proving myself forever. Whatever I did, there would never be any question of me being given a key.

In the mornings Ray marched me downstairs and opened the front door to let me out. One day early in my stay I noticed there was mail on the mat and I bent down to pick it up. Ray didn't say anything to discourage me, he simply trod on the little pile of letters as a way of telling me to keep my hands to myself. He was always very direct. He wouldn't tell you something if he could simply show you.

In my memory his every footfall had a metallic echo—there were heel plates on his bike boots to reduce wear. From time to time he must have gone barefoot, maybe he was even barefoot when he trod on the mail to declare it out of bounds. Maybe it's a false memory that supplies the crunching boot, descending so finally on something that was none of my business.

My first job, as you'd expect, had been helping out in the chemist's during school holidays. I even enjoyed it. It was only a few years since Mum and Dad's shop sold sweets from big glass jars. Sometimes when I was working there I'd close my eyes and think I could still smell them, the acid drops and the liquorice. I'd think I could reach out my hand and touch the big jars.

At primary school I'd said that I lived in a sweet shop, and when my classmates wanted to come to tea, either because they believed me or because they didn't, I said my parents had been killed. Run over by a lorry while they crossed the road at a dangerous place. Which made my class sympathetic for a day and mocking after that.

Dad wasn't a very businesslike businessman. It was a full year after decimalization that he gave in to Mum's urgings and got a decimal till. Till then he must have thought that the new currency was no more than a fad, and shillings and pence would come back again once everyone had tired of the outlandish new coins. It was like county names. Technically Middlesex had stopped existing a couple of years before, and now everything was part of Greater London. But everyone just kept on putting Middlesex on letters, and ignoring postcodes, which had come in a little earlier.

So I suppose Dad's rebellion against decimalization was part of a larger thing. We would do the sums in our heads, pressing down any key of the old preelectric till to make the money drawer shoot out. People could still do mental arithmetic then, not feeling faint when more than two numbers need to be added up, helpless without a calculator.

In the 1970s, a family chemist's was still a viable business. The supermarkets hadn't really started to siphon off the toiletry trade, and the pharmacy side of things offered a service they didn't even try to match. It's absurd to think how restricted our stock was, looking back: some posh perfume for Christmas and people who'd forgotten their wives' birthdays, a couple of brands of shampoo. There just wasn't the range then, and people wouldn't be conditioner conscious for years to come. Dentists had only just stopped telling people to brush from side to side, and now it was the heyday of up-and-down. We hadn't been told to brush in one direction only yet, away from the gum, let alone to brush in little circles.

Everything was old-fashioned, though of course that didn't occur to me then. It was what I knew. When people came into the shop, a primitive mechanism made a bell ring, with a click that was almost louder than the ding it produced. The shop had only the most basic security: a household lock on the front door, another one on the pharmacy storeroom. It didn't occur to us in Isleworth at the time that people might want to break in and steal drugs to use or sell. But then I remember the time when Kaolin & Morphine, which you bought over the counter, still had plenty of morphine in it, so anybody who seriously wanted to be stupefied didn't need to try very hard.

This was before specialized shops for developing film. Everyone took their snaps to the chemist's. Anything quicker than a week counted as an Express Service and called for extra paperwork. Hardly anyone asked for it, and if they did we'd wonder why. Why would people want their holiday snaps back in such a hurry? More than likely it was just swank and showing off. A way of making out that you were important people and everything about you was urgent, even your holidays.

I'd have been happy to go on working in the chemist's, but Dad wasn't happy to have me there. At first I thought it was because he'd be embarrassed to have me sell condoms to a customer. We had a few customers who bought Durex, and one who must have been allergic to latex, since we kept the special lambskin ones in stock for him. But eventually I realized that Dad was even embarrassed to serve those customers himself, when I was in the shop.

By the time I met Ray I was a trainee gardener for the Council, working mainly in Lampton Park over in Hounslow, a bus ride away from home and no great distance from Hampton. Isleworth is only a hop skip and a jump from Kew Gardens, but I'd never set my sights that high. I'm just not cut out for it. The big league.

People who've done a little weekend digging and mowing always think it would be great to be a gardener for a living. All that fresh air. I suppose it might be more satisfying nowadays—ideas about what makes a good park have moved on, though these days of course all the work is put out to private tender, so someone like me would never get a crack at it.

In those days there were no wild areas in parks. Everything was regimented and symmetry was all the trend. You might spend days planting begonias in perfectly regular lines and rows, though if you like flowers you probably don't like straight lines. If you were mowing the bowling green you wouldn't expect the work to be anything but repetitive, but everything seemed to be like that.

We trainees worked under a Mr. Jarvis—Mikey behind his back. We thought of him as a terrible old ponce, though I suppose he was only in his late thirties, younger than I am now, and he was more pathetic than anything else. He was easy to make fun of, having hair growing out of his ears and nostrils, and I can't say I was above the temptation to play along with the others. There were poofter jokes too which I didn't have the courage to challenge or take the sting out of. Well, you don't when you're eighteen, do you? If it wasn't him it would certainly be me. The other trainees made no end of fun of me when my hairstyle changed. My new look was a bit drastic.

Mikey Jarvis's previous job had been in the Royal Parks, and he was always comparing everything with those glory days: the equipment, the human resources. The human resources, meaning us. He was forever telling us about the time he drove his tractor down Piccadilly to Fortnum & Mason to pick up a vast pottery jar of something called Gentleman's Relish for Her Majesty the Queen Mother (it's fish paste), and the times that gracious lady in person toddled across the lawns of Clarence House with a glass of beer in her hands—a full pint, mind you, not a half—to say "Happy Birthday Mr. Jarvis." Apparently she's a great one for those sorts of touches.

Of course since Mikey was always boasting about the past, we wondered what he could have done to end up in Lampton Park, which he clearly saw as a sort of Siberia of gardening where he would toil and die. We decided he must have arranged plants in some pornographic pattern, or used fertilizer to spell out obscenities on the lawns. We did that a lot ourselves, spelling out COUNCIL PAY IS SHIT in yellow tulips against red for the entertainment of passing helicopters. As far as Mikey's disgrace was concerned, we wasted a lot of time trying to work out what message had got him into trouble. The idea that cracked us up the most was PRINCESS ANNE LOVES HORSES, spelled out somewhere it could be read from the Palace.

In winter gardeners work short hours, and then Ray's rules affected me more. It was like a curfew only in reverse—not being allowed home until a certain time. But there was always Hounslow Library to spend time in, though you can't spend more than an hour or two in a library without feeling that the staff see you as a borderline tramp. The bus connections were pretty good back them, though people still complained, just for the practice. And I could always visit Mum and Dad in Isleworth, in the house that I had a key to. Most of my books were there anyway. Ray allowed me half a shelf in Hampton for books, on condition that I took in exchange a pile of old martial arts magazines that he wasn't yet ready to throw away. There wasn't any spare shelf room, so that was the only way it could have worked, really, by our exchanging a block of books.

Ray could throw out my naff toiletries and keep me out of the house during the day, and he didn't need to give a reason. That was just the way it was. So what if the cleaning lady had more privileges than I did, seeing as she could let herself in with a key every Thursday? Maybe I felt a little resentment of the cleaning lady and her key, all the same, resentment I wasn't even aware of. One Thursday morning I left the bed unmade, thinking she was going to be changing the sheets anyway, so what was the point of putting myself out for no reason? That was one of the few times I ever saw Ray angry. He talked about how fucking inconsiderate I was being, till I wondered if maybe he had been brought up with servants, to be so concerned about their working conditions. After that first night I didn't sleep in the bed anyway unless Ray needed me, but I was perfectly comfortable in the sleeping bag on the floor. I got good rest there.

If I'd wanted to delve into Ray's belongings, I could easily have done that on a Saturday morning. His bike-cleaning routine was so unvarying and protracted. And yet my feeling for him didn't include curiosity. I felt it was right that I should have no privacy, since I had no secrets from him. And I needed him to have his privacy, because I needed him to have secrets. His central secret for me, of course, being not why he didn't give me a key, but why he let me stay at all. It was a question I didn't want answered. It couldn't be good for me to know.

It wasn't that I didn't have ordinary curiosity about ordinary things. When I was working in the chemist's and I was alone for a bit, I'd work methodically through the photos waiting to be collected. I'd hold them carefully by the edges, anxious not to take the bloom off the emulsion. I don't know what I was looking for, exactly, but it seems to be true that other people's holidays are a blur of happiness, and the sun follows them wherever they go.

So if I wasn't curious about Ray, there was a bit of philosophy behind it. In fairy stories, I know you're supposed to sympathize with the person who can't resist asking the fatal question, make the fatal discovery, but I never did. I mean, Mrs. Bluebeard wasn't really on the ball, if she thought she'd settled down with a man who had no secrets. If all the doors in the spooky castle had been unlocked, if she could wander wherever she wished, her husband would never have appealed to her. He would have been just another smoothie she met at a party. Another smooth Duke with a house too big for two people, hard to keep warm in the wintertime.

When a year had gone by and I was about to be nineteen, I realized that Ray must have had a birthday of his own somewhere along the way, without letting on. He wouldn't even own up to a definite age, a birth year, and he didn't enjoy those sorts of questions. So I decided that my birthday would have to be his official birthday as well. In fact we needed to crowd three celebrations into a single day, since it was our anniversary to boot. I always played safe with my presents. I usually gave him a book, once I was confident that I knew his tastes. We spent some of our happiest times at the flat in Cardinals Paddock just sitting there, both of us reading. He even asked for a particular book about jewelery once, a big and expensive book, and it was a surprise because he never wore any. You couldn't count the sort of half bangles he had in summer, a band of tan on the upper part of each wrist, where the sun fell on the skin between glove edge and jacket cuff. He didn't wear gauntlets—not even in winter. There's always something overdone about bike gauntlets, they're too obvious an armor, they make you look feeble somehow.

He'd have his feet up on a stool, and I would sit between his legs, knowing not to annoy him by propping my book on his boots. The creak of his leathers, so close, was like the creak of a ship's rigging, so that I could believe I was on a journey. He'd squeeze my neck with those mighty legs of his just hard enough to keep me thinking of him.

There'd be music on the stereo, more often one of his big tapes rather than an LP. The sound quality wasn't so good but he didn't have to get up so often to change it. I didn't know much about classical music before Ray, but thanks to him I broadened out quite a bit. Thanks to him I learned that the pretty tune I always thought went with the words *I've Got A Ferret Sticking Up My Nose* is actually the middle section of the Slow Movement of Chopin's Piano Sonata in B flat. Part of the funeral march.

I even learned to tolerate jazz, of the moody sort Ray liked so much, though it always bothered me that a nice little tune like "My Favorite Things" out of *The Sound Of Music* could last half an hour, if it fell into the wrong hands.

And what did I give him in return? Well, I taught him not

to take books for granted, the outsides of books as well as the insides, their bindings. It was his only real bit of untidiness, and I schooled him out of it, just by example, not by saying anything. When I met him he would leave books open and face down, but inside a couple of years he was a reformed character.

I didn't tell him how I learned to be so scrupulous with objects. It wasn't from records, from my "collection," and he didn't let me touch his. What LPs did I have to protect from sticky marks except *School's Out* and *Nursery Cryme*? I got into the habit of holding books gently, opening them only a little way, peering at the text as if I had no right, from sneaking peeks at people's snaps at the chemist's in Isleworth, knowing better than to leave smudges on their memories.

Every now and then Ray would step up the pressure, crossing his ankles to get more leverage, until my ears roared and the print faded from in front of my eyes. That was exciting. If it didn't happen for a while, I'd find myself pressing backwards against his groin, knowing that he might just get annoyed with me, but unable to stop myself trying for a reaction. I think Ray was proud of my endurance. There was one time he was a bit relentless and I started to pass out, and after that maybe I'd built up the strength of my neck and maybe he was a little bit easier on me. But not so much easier that I felt disappointed.

On my twentieth birthday I gave him his present, saying, "Happy Official Birthday, Raymond," and he didn't exactly scowl, but he was a long way from smiling, and he said, "What makes you think my name is Raymond? Maybe it's just Ray." It may have been that he was just being gruff because he'd planned a birthday surprise, *Carmen*. Not my top favorite opera—I like all the business about fate, but if you've actually known someone who changes her mind and won't change it back, had one in the family, then you don't find it all that thrilling to see the same thing up on stage. So not my top favorite opera, but still a huge treat.

I was wearing a nice suit, jangling coins in my pocket very happily, when Ray came out of the bedroom wearing his idea of evening dress suitable for a night at the opera. It was exactly what he would wear on a bike run, except that instead of a black leather shirt he wore one in tan leather, which laced up to the neck. That was the fashion then. For once I felt so very much the birthday boy that without thinking of the risk I was taking I blurted out, "You're not taking me to the opera dressed like that!" I know. Like the mother in a sitcom. Big risk to be taking.

I'm not a snoop and I don't pry, unless you count the holiday snaps of strangers, but in the cupboard in Ray's bedroom in full view hung five beautiful suits—two gray, two cream, one brown. Was it asking so much to want him to dress down for me?

He gave me a truly poisonous look, but no, apparently it wasn't so very much to ask. He slammed the bedroom door behind him, mind you, and he made me wait. He wanted me to think he was pulling a huge sulk, that he wasn't ever coming out. But by then I felt I had the measure of the man. And sure enough, he came out all nonchalant in one of the creams. Looking absolutely fantastic. Before he phoned for the cab he said, "You know you'll pay for this later," and by then I knew him well enough to say, "I'll remind you." On the night of my birthday, of our birthday, Ray let me sleep in the bed, so I really was taking a risk, though all in all I slept better on the floor.

There were other surprises that took more getting used to than opera tickets on my birthday. One Saturday night while the poker club was in session, I was sitting there cross-legged reading my book when I looked up. I was trying to make sense of the Thirty Years' War, which wasn't that easy even during the thirty years that the war lasted. It took me a little moment to find my bearings in the present day, and to focus on what was in front of me.

In front of me was a pair of boots, but they weren't Ray's. Ray wore Gold Tops, the sort motorcycle policemen wear—he was very proud of them—and these were Doc Martens, which weren't acceptable on a bike run but passed muster on a Saturday night. And if the boots weren't Ray's, then it followed that the cock sticking out of the jeans a little above my eye level wasn't Ray's either. Not Ray's at all. It had a different shape and a different size and a different slant. Different animal altogether.

Paul stood there as if he was waiting for me to service him, staring flatly down at me in a way that I suppose was an imitation of Ray, and I honestly didn't know what to do. I looked over to Ray, but he was concentrating on his poker hand and didn't look up. Of course it was just me-in-the-window, him-cleaning-the-bike all over again. He knew perfectly well that I wanted some guidance, and he was letting me know that I'd have to make the decision without his help. I was on my own. I was standing at a crossroads where there were no signposts.

I just didn't know what was the right thing to do. Ray was entitled to use me as and when he pleased, and if his poker hand folded and he wanted me to suck his cock until the next hand was dealt, then that was his privilege. I was well used to that. But didn't I belong to him and him only? Wasn't that the bargain that was struck the first night I spent with Ray, the night he took possession? The trouble with contracts made without a word being said is that you never have a chance to read the small print.

I was afraid that if I opened my mouth and got to work on Paul, the way he so obviously expected me to, I'd spoil things between me and Ray forever, and all for something I didn't especially want to do. But if Ray had told Paul that he could help himself, then I would make him look bad in front of the club.

I didn't refuse Paul, but it was obvious that I was unsure and hesitating. He called over to the poker table, "Ray?" Ray didn't look up, and his tone of voice when he drawled "Yeah?" was somehow silky, which I took to be a bad sign. Right there and then I had the sinking feeling that I had made the wrong choice. I was already moving past the unsignposted crossroads, on a conveyor belt. I was already heading down the wrong fork.

Paul's cock was still hanging there in front of me while he carried on a little conversation with the group behind his back. He waggled his hips slightly, so that his cock waggled also, either with the idea of tempting me, or the way that some people wag a finger to mean *naughty naughty*. Paul said, "Ray, is this boy of yours on strike?"

And Ray said, lazily, drawling the words, "Not that I know of." Letting a little silence form. "Not unless he joined the union since this morning." Still he kept his eyes on the cards in his hand. So of course I had to open up to Paul, which was suddenly a relief since it meant that I didn't have to look at the stupid grin of triumph on his face.

And that was how I learned that if this was some sort of commune, then I was part of what it shared in common. All for one, and Colin for everybody. Colin on demand. The crack about unions was definitely a punishment, I thought, for my wavering. A bit of a low blow. There was a lot of union-bashing around in the late seventies, before Thatcher came in. You could hardly open a paper without reading about how the unions were bringing the country to its knees with their lunatic demands—only I never thought so.

Ray knew full well I was a union man, and he'd heard me say time and time that a strike was a measure of last resort and not what the trades union movement was really about. He even knew that the thing I liked least about Saturday nights was hearing the members of the poker club make ill-informed comments on that sort of subject, and not be able to put my point of view. It was a real test of character for me, curled up on the floor, trying to concentrate on my book, and of course not allowed to speak unless spoken to by a member. So Ray was really hitting me where it hurt, hitting below the belt, when he made that remark.

It was a bad moment. Of course I'd let Ray down in public—my hesitation had damaged him momentarily in the eyes of the group—so he was only retaliating, really. And after that I knew not to hesitate, and I made sure he never needed to feel ashamed of me again.

In practice, the fellows only wanted to make use of me if they'd folded in the game, until the next deal, so it wasn't hard work. Nobody worried in those days where come went or didn't go, but usually they saved themselves for later on. Sometimes a fellow would want his arse licked instead of a blow job, and I'd be lying if I said I was always raring to go. But even when things got tedious, and I was basically waiting for bluffs to be called, debts settled, and the arrival of the next deal, wanting only to get back to my book, it was still better than Wolf Cubs.

In about two years, I got some company. I don't mean to say that Ray wasn't company. I mean company on Saturday nights. Bob got himself a boy of his own. Kevin. Bob used to say, "I saw him advertised in a magazine. I sent for him by mail order"—the same way Ray used to say, "Colin didn't fall *for* me, he fell *over* me."

What Bob said was even pretty much true. None of the club members read the gay press, such as it was in those days, but you could get away with an amazing amount in the Personals column of *Motor Cycle News*.

There were a lot of paradoxes like that in those days, bits of latitude in the system. So you couldn't get porn, however soft—or that's what people said—but you hardly needed to, when *Films and Filming* was there in stacks in every newsagent, with bare chests on every page and a few bottoms thrown in for luck. Hardly a woman to be seen. Someone on the staff must have had a real thing about one particular actor, someone called Jan-Michael Vincent. I've never heard of any of the films he starred in, perhaps they were made up, but he starred in a lot of people's teenage dreams, thank to *Films and Filming*. *Shirts and Shirtlifters*, people called it. It was so blatant.

Somebody at *Motor Cycle News* must have turned a blind eye to the Personals. There was a sort of code involved, but it wasn't like the code that won the war. No maths required. It was perfectly obvious if you were looking for it. Dominant, submissive: they weren't personality profiles, exactly. They meant something a little different from extrovert, introvert.

A year or two later *MCN* cracked down on the code, but you could still read that confident blokes were looking for shy mates and so on. The strong-minded were still looking for the suggestible. Ray was funny about it, imagining a time when you'd have to say, "Decisive biker seeks vague pillion." But the message would still get across, one way or another. People will always find each other.

At first I didn't take to Kevin, I'm ashamed to say, because he was an absolute sweetheart. The reason I didn't take to him was I suppose because he was even younger than me, and I suppose pretty. In fact definitely pretty. I was bound to worry if he was going to become the favorite. And Kevin had ribs. The only way anybody's every going to see my ribs is with an X-ray machine. You have to take my ribs on trust, but Kevin's were there for the world to see.

I was confident that Ray wasn't going to transfer his interest to someone new, but I also knew he had two sides to him, the private citizen and the unofficial club president, and he would hardly take kindly to the eclipse of his own mascot.

There was a bit more to it, if I'm honest. Kevin was a punk, and he had one of those very elaborate punky hairstyles, covering only a stripe of his head like what's called a mohican, only dyed red and formed into spikes. This was a style called a cockatoo.

It just seemed unfair that he was allowed to keep that fancy hairstyle. I'd spent two years of Saturday nights down there on the floor, and just when someone was supposed to be joining me there, it turned out he had special privileges from the word go. We weren't being treated equally. When you're naked and on display, and one of you has hair and the other doesn't—any hair, let alone an eye-catching set of scarlet spokes—that's a clear advantage. You could say that the one with the cockatoo hairstyle is still secretly wearing something. Not being truly naked.

Ray cut my hair short the week after I moved in, cut it all

off more or less, which was an improvement in some ways, I expect, or he wouldn't have done it. But I always felt that having super short hair, more like scalp-stubble really, made my ears look sticky-out, and I never quite got used to the bumps I felt when I put my hand up above the hairline. My little Mum was always pleading with me to grow it back, even just a bit, and I couldn't really explain that it wasn't up to me. It was something that my little Dad agreed with her about, and they couldn't see why I was being so stubborn. They both saw Ray as a good influence, and it wouldn't have been right to let them know that he was responsible for the only change in me they didn't like.

So I felt quite resentful of Kevin. I mean, it's one thing to make things easier for a newcomer to the group, but shouldn't Paul have made it clear that the hair had to go? And failing that, shouldn't Ray have made a ruling? Paul would hardly have put up a fight if Ray had laid down the law.

And it didn't stop there. From the very first Saturday night, Kevin had his say in choosing some of the music. Of course his choice was punky stuff, but that wasn't the bit that upset me. When punks first appeared I was scared of them, but that soon passed, even if I don't remember ever actually thinking they were sexy. In any case, after a while his taste changed and he began to fit in more with the group. He brought along heavy metal. Which I didn't like much better, I have to say. But the thing was, nobody ever asked me if there was music I wanted to choose for Saturday nights. And I understood why, but it still bothered me that Kevin seemed to have such a smooth ride.

Ray liked chamber music, Ray liked arty songs as well as jazz of the moody sort. But when he listened to music, he liked to give it his full attention. He didn't want to be doing anything else, unless it was music he knew well and he was reading a book. So he never exercised his right to choose poker-club music, which meant that there was no chance of me getting a look in. My refusal was taken for granted, it went along automatically with his. Yes, of course, I might have embarrassed myself. Certainly there were some disco songs I liked at the time, and a little gentle reggae, that might not have gone down too well. And if I'd had my choices, I might have cringed looking back on them now. But I couldn't help feeling I had the right to give it a go.

I was building up a low-key grievance against Ray for letting Kevin get away with things, which is bound to poison any relationship unless it's dealt with promptly. It doesn't do to let things fester. But he handled it in the most magnificent way, without a word said, at least to me. He left just the right amount of time. He waited until the fourth poker night, when Kevin was settling in and could expect a little attention from him.

Ray folded his poker hand, went over to Kevin and unzipped. Kevin looked up at him with a great grin, and my heart sank. Kevin was ready, Kevin was better than ready. Kevin was pretty much wagging his tail. This was what he had been waiting for. And yet Ray never got involved. It wasn't the way Kevin must have hoped. It wasn't a case of the beautiful biker man feeding his hard-on to the pretty new boy whose ribs you can actually see. It was dutiful, somehow. It was like a club formality. It wasn't intense. It was like Prince Philip opening a hospital annex.

While Kevin was worshipping his cock, Ray kept his hips from moving, and I noticed he even folded his hands together behind his back. Just like Prince Philip. If he'd been a smoker I swear he'd have lit up a cigarette. Then he politely pulled out, without the pat on the back that Kevin might have thought he'd earned. And came over to me.

He gave me my chance to shine. By now the other members were ready for another deal of poker, but he kept on going, pumping his cock into my mouth. He closed his eyes. He was telling them that tonight he didn't care about the cards. For once the cards could wait. The poker club could wait until he was good and ready, even though the album side I'd come to recognize as Deep Purple had finished. Then when the members were getting restless, he did a sort of double take. He didn't come, that would have been too obvious. But he opened his eyes.

Every time I saw him again, Ray's eyes were bluer than I remembered them, even if I had seen him the day before and spent the night with him. I wondered if his eyes weren't actually luminous, so that blue built up behind the lids when he was asleep. And I'd try to be awake before him, so that I could catch the moment when the pent-up blue spilled out.

Ray suddenly stopped and opened his eyes, and he said, almost dreamily, "I'm sorry, am I keeping people waiting? I must have lost track of time." Then he made the gesture that would have been ruffling my hair, if I'd had more hair, and zipped himself up. Then he murmured, "I was thinking about something else," and calmly went back to the poker table.

So I was left sweaty and dribbling, also deeply happy and vindicated. Ray had really shown Kevin what was what. He'd really put him in his place by fucking my face.

And in point of fact Kevin was a sweetheart. I really warmed to him once we got used to each other. Technically, as neither of us actually belonged to the club, and each of us could only speak if addressed by a member, conversation between us was impossible, but Kevin found his way round that little difficulty. Even though I, I'm ashamed to say, would have been content to keep everything chilly and correct. Some way short of cordial, looking over from my thermos of tea and my history book at his bottle of Coke and *New Musical Express*. Diet Coke hadn't been invented then.

Kevin stuck his tongue out. At first I was scandalized and offended, thinking he was simply being rude. Paul had just finished with him to go back to the poker game, and I thought this was just rivalry and defiance. His way of saying, I'm being taken care of. I'm being looked after just as well as you. To stop me getting above myself.

But it wasn't that at all. He had nerve, that one. I noticed he was doing something funny with his eyes. He was crossing them, making out that he was looking down on that extended tongue. Then he made an exaggerated pounce with a pair of pinching fingers down onto his tongue. All this while Paul was hardly back in the game, and could look over at him at any moment. Paul who had quite a temper on him. And Kevin was miming finding one of Paul's ginger hairs glinting on his tongue with a grimace to show how little he appreciated it being left there. It was his way of making peace. Making things all right between us, and letting me know he wanted us to be friends.

He didn't have to do that, but I was glad that he did. We were careful not to be noticed by the membership, but there was a little flicker of communication going between Kevin and me the whole time. Saturday nights had a whole new dimension, suddenly. We would mime having our fingers crossed that Alan's poker hand would be good or his bluffing inspired. If he folded his hand and came towards us, we'd look away, me at the Roman Empire or the First World War, him at the reviews of Clash concerts, each despite our new connection hoping that he would choose the other. Then afterwards the lucky one would send rueful looks to the unlucky one, or if we were feeling really daring mime being sick. Alan wasn't clean. He was the only one who wasn't. Alan's cock tasted of stale piss and neither of us wanted it, ever.

Then one night Alan tried to fuck my arse, and Ray threw him downstairs. I wasn't supposed to leave my post unless it was to run an errand for a member, which was why I had a thermos for my tea, but Alan sent me to fetch some beer from the kitchen, and then he cornered me there. After the earlier embarrassment, I wasn't even sure he hadn't the right to fuck me—I *thought* I knew he didn't, but it had never been said, and I didn't dare to cry out, but I managed to knock the dustbin over, sending some bottles rolling, and that came to the same thing. Ray came flying in, no words just action. I think he'd have thrown Alan downstairs even it was Alan who was playing host that night and they were *his* stairs, which thank God they weren't or the repercussions for the club would have been much nastier. We were at Big Steve's place in West Byfleet.

We never saw Alan again. For all I know he was the best poker player on God's earth, but Kevin and I never missed him. Afterwards Ray stroked my head to comfort me, and asked me the same question he always asked and always answered in the same way. Not "What am I going to do with you?" which he'd pretty much demonstrated month by month, but "Why did I take you on?" He always supplied an answer of his own to that question. The answer he gave was always, "No one else would have you."

It's true there's never been a queue. But Ray always seemed

to be getting at something else, with that question and that answer, as if there was something he needed me to understand. Looking at it sensibly, if no one else would have me, if I wasn't any sort of prize, then that should be a reason for Ray to stay away too. He could have anyone he wanted, with his looks and his personality. So: how did it come about that it was a good thing and not a bad one that I had no other options? I tried not to think about it too much. It might not be a good idea for me to know Ray's reasons. I was a bit superstitious about that. I didn't want to jinx things.

This is how I worked it out. My value to him was my loyalty. I belonged to him. Loyalty wasn't just one virtue among others, it was the only virtue in the world as far as he was concerned. It made me worth having, which meant that before me, someone in the past must have let him down. There must have been someone who hadn't been told "No one else would have you," or who'd found someone else who would, and who'd just moved on after all Ray's devotion, after the effort he had put in.

It made a sort of sense. Maybe Ray had learned a horrible lesson, and that's why he had drawn such a clear line, I mean by not letting me have a key to where he lived. Maybe a boy before me who nobody talked about, a silly lad who broke his heart, if that's what happened, had taken advantage and just expected to be looked after. Not to lift a finger. So Ray was going to make sure it didn't happen again. It was funny to think that Ray, who lived in the present like no one I've known, might have been shaped by the past in a small way.

It wouldn't be right to say that Ray held me back. It would be ungrateful and wrong. But it's a fact that I wouldn't have been able to work shifts, the way I do now, if I was still with Ray. Fifteen years I've been on the road now. I wasn't cut out to be a gardener, and I knew that even then. But I couldn't have been on early turn or late turn at work and still fitted in with Ray's schedule. Ray's life.

Six years I had with Ray. We'd celebrated my twenty-fourth birthday, which meant he was certainly thirty, but not yet thirty-five. Then like a fool I went on holiday with Mum and Dad. Worst decision I ever made. But they asked me to go. Joyce was supposed to go with them, but then she was suddenly pregnant after years of trying, and it would be a mistake to travel in that condition. And it was beginning to become clear that Mum and Dad really needed someone to go with them. They even let me choose the details of the trip.

Mum was soon on her feet after her hospital stay in 1975. The polyps meant her no harm, just like we'd been told, though they needed to be checked every now and then. Everything seemed to be back to normal, and it took all of us a good long time to understand that nothing would ever be the same again.

The difference was all in my little Dad. It wasn't just his hair going white, his whole outlook changed. He and Mum were still inseparable, but it wasn't the same kind of inseparable. The balance went out of it. Balance went, and fear came in. It wasn't any more that they dealt with life instinctively as a couple, although they were always together. It was simply that he couldn't bear to let her out of his sight, which seemed the same at first but was almost the opposite.

Soon we noticed, Joyce and me, that Dad was becoming absentminded, but in a way that was anxious rather than vague. He would fret if Mum so much as left the room, as if he didn't know where she was unless he could actually see her. He'd ask, "Where's your Mum?" trying to sound unconcerned, and if we said, "Don't you know? Do you really not know?" he'd say, "In the kitchen," or "In the bathroom," with an uncertain edge to his voice that we weren't meant to notice if he guessed right. Usually he guessed right. Then everything was supposed to be back to normal. He'd manage to stay calm as long as she came back into the room before too long. The funny thing was that he never actually went looking for her, he wanted to stay where he was, he just wanted her to be there too. So his behavior had two things in it, the needing her to be there and the not wanting to go anywhere.

Another funny thing was that if he knew she was there, he stopped paying attention to her. If she was drying her hair with her old-fashioned pink plastic hairdryer—I don't know why she didn't pick up something more up-to-date from the shop—then he knew that as long as the whirring noise went on she was still there, and he'd close his eyes and seem to doze until the noise stopped.

I don't know whose idea it was that Dad should retire a couple of years early. Perhaps he wasn't up to doing the job any more. Maybe he couldn't concentrate properly on filling prescriptions, even though Mum was in the shop with him. Of course Dad made out that nothing was wrong, and Mum wouldn't say anything about how it was that might sound like criticism, even to me. But maybe he kept looking at her, and when he brought his attention back to the prescription form, which someone was waiting for, it was as if he'd never seen the piece of paper in his hand before.

At first retirement seemed to suit Dad fine. He was quite happy at home, as long as Mum left a note saying she was working in the shop. First of all she would put it in his jacket pocket, but then she learned to pin it to the outside of the jacket instead. If she left it loose, it might end up on the floor, and then he'd be very agitated by the time she came back for lunch, or after work. He'd say, "Where have you been all day?" but if she said, "Where do you think I've been?" he'd say, "At work, of course. In the shop." It was strange. When Mum started taking Dad to doctors, they agreed that Dad wasn't becoming demented. That wasn't the problem.

The crumbling of Dad's behavior was all to do with Mum and her whereabouts. Apart from that, his mental powers were no different. He knew what day it was, who was Prime Minister—in fact, he could reel them off in reverse order, with dates, all the way back to Pitt. He even kept up with new drugs and brand names though he didn't work more than the occasional Sunday shift in the shop, as the pharmacy rota prompted. If the new pharmacist took ill or had time off, Dad could hold the fort, just as long as Mum stood near him, and didn't serve a customer while he was filling a prescription. Sundays weren't usually that busy. Dad was all there mentally, as long as Mum was right there beside him.

Mum wouldn't let on how all this got her down, but you didn't need ESP to realize that she really needed to get away. So I fell in with this idea of a holiday in France, nipping across on the hovercraft early in the summer season. Even Dad liked the idea of the hovercraft, a British invention and stylish and fun. I'd also been reading Geoffrey of Monmouth, and I took it into my head to visit some of the places he mentions in France. Geoffrey—or Galfridus as he called himself, writing in Latin, Galfridus Monemutensis—isn't most people's idea of a historian, but some things that seem fanciful in his writings turn out to be true. True-ish, at any rate. So he talks about how Merlin brought Stonehenge to Salisbury Plain from Mount Killaraus in Ireland, which isn't so different from where archaeologists these days reckon the stones came from. And he talks about how the Venedoti decapitated an entire Roman legion in London and threw their heads into a stream. And what was found in the bed of the Walbrook in the 1860s but a large number of skulls? With practically no other bones to keep them company.

So I was excited despite myself to read Geoffrey of Monmouth on Arthur's last battle, about Kay the Seneschal being carried dying to Chinon, the town he himself had built. About Bedivere the Cupbearer, borne with loud lamentation to Bayeux, the city his grandfather had founded, where he was laid to rest "beside a wall in a certain cemetery in the Southern quarter of the city." I didn't expect to trip over the bones of a Grail Knight, the way I'd tripped over Ray's foot at Box Hill, but I really wanted to visit those towns, and to snuffle up the distant whiff of events from long ago.

Of course it wasn't like that. We made a sort of visit to Bayeux, but for most of the holiday Dad stayed in the hotel. He didn't want to go anywhere. It turned out that he felt unsteady coming downstairs, and so he sat down on the top step and wouldn't come down any further. That's where he stayed, and he wanted Mum to stay there too. I led Dad back to the room and persuaded Mum to come out with me, that first day. Dad was afraid that someone would try to talk French to him while Mum wasn't there, even though all the staff spoke excellent English, so we left the phrase book behind just to pacify him. Somehow it wasn't there when we got back—God knows what he'd done with it—so the next day the pressure on Mum to stay was more intense.

Mum arranged a swap of rooms, so that she and Dad were

on the ground floor, but then it turned out he felt just as un-steady on the three steps that led down from the hotel lobby into the street.

I was only away with Mum and Dad for ten days, but that was enough to finish six years. Not just to put an end to them, but to make them disappear. When I got back it was a Wednes-day. In the evening I phoned the Hampton flat. Mum and Dad finally had a phone by then, but there were no answering ma-chines in 1981. I mean they existed, but nobody had one. No-body in Isleworth or Hampton anyway. When I got no answer, I started worrying immediately. Ray was nothing if not reli-able. I rang every hour that evening, and before nine the next morning. I kept up that pattern every day, even though I knew after the Wednesday that I'd have to wait until Sunday to find anything out. Sunday at Box Hill, where the bikers go.

It was a terrible week for Mum as well as for me. Of course it was. She couldn't pretend after France that life with Dad was ever going to be again what it had been. A partnership. She'd been abroad for ten days, and more than a week of that had been spent in a hotel room keeping her husband calm. Reas-suring him that she wasn't going to leave him alone—that she went on existing quite reliably even if a door happened to close between them.

But Mum knew what I was going through, too, and she asked Joyce to come round and sit with Dad for an hour on the Sunday, pregnancy or no pregnancy, so that she could give me a lift to Box Hill. Box Hill, where the bikers go to show themselves off.

In my memory, there was a huge thundercloud hanging over Box Hill, like the doom cloud after a nuclear explosion, but my diary tells me the sky was clear. The doom cloud arrived later, with Big Steve and Little Steve. Disaster rode pillion with them.

Mum let me off by the café at the bottom. That was where most people looked in. Before she left she told me to have a cup of coffee—I wouldn't miss my friends, they'd be looking for me just as surely as I was looking for them. Which was true, but I couldn't have kept down even a cup of coffee. And I worried that if the club arrived as a group they'd go straight up the hill and not stop by the café. Even though I knew the club would not be arriving in full force. The club's force was spent. There was a signboard covered with advertisements for bikes and bike gear, pillions wanting rides, hard-to-find spare parts for the British bikes that you saw on the roads less and less. If I'd closed my eyes I might have been able to tell a difference in the general engine noise from the first time I'd gone there— the contribution made by the trail bikes that were coming into fashion, with their angry chainsaw revving. The aggressive names that were going to be fashionable, Dominator, Virago, Intruder. None of the quiet authority of Commando.

I knew that if no one came I'd end up climbing the hill on foot, though there would really be no point. If Ray arrived, leading the pack, carrying the spare helmet for me, he'd pull in by the café. I'd see him, and he'd see me. He'd be quite capable of driving past me as if I was invisible, until he was good and ready to acknowledge me, but he'd see me all right.

Of course when Big Steve and Little Steve pulled in on their machines, I tried not to see them. If they were there without Ray, then there was nothing to be hoped for. While they dismounted and started to come heavily towards me, I turned away. I couldn't run, I was just stumbling away from the news they brought. They caught me up and they held on to me. In a way, that was the most awful moment: if their wish to comfort me was an indication of my loss then I was desolate. It wasn't the way I was used to being handled by the bike club. It wasn't the treatment their mascot normally received. I felt trapped. Claustrophobic, as if I was held in a suffocating space, where there was no breath to be had. I shut my eyes, and if they hadn't been holding my arms I'd have put my hands over my ears.

Ray lived life like no one else I've ever heard of, but there was absolutely nothing distinctive about his death. A tree. A patch of oil and a tree. A hairpin bend, a patch of oil and a tree.

The bikers in the club were always philosophical about two-wheeled risk. Spend time on a bike and you'll spend some of that time sliding off it. But I'd taken it for granted that Ray was immune, the same way he was the only one of them who never seemed to have a plastic bag blow onto his hot exhaust pipes, melting with a stench and taking hours to clean off.

The guidelines seemed to be, from what they said: Lose as much speed as you can. If you're heading towards a car, aim for the lowest part, the bonnet or boot rather than the body. Relax.

None of which would have made any difference to Ray. It made no difference, come to that, that he'd done all his checks. His tires were inflated to the correct pressure front and rear, and his brakes bit with useless crispness as the bike slid sideways towards the tree. The bike was highly polished at the moment of his losing control of it. It made no difference that Ray had made the prescribed observations with turns of the head, not relying on his mirrors, as he approached the bend that he wouldn't see the end of.

He was doing less than thirty miles an hour. From what the Steves said, it might only have been twenty. Usually a bike and its master part company quite sweetly in the course of an accident, following separate trajectories, and in the first half second after Ray lost control that's what happened to him. The inexperienced rider clutches at the machine, the seasoned one knows to let it go. The seasoned rider waves it farewell. But the connection between the two of them was too strong to be broken so easily. Somehow the bike righted itself, the engine still running, and rammed him against the tree. Of course he didn't look up at the last instant, to be dazzled while he died by the headlight he kept switched on day and night for safety's sake. That was just a picture in my mind.

When I'd absorbed the first shock, I was still a mess. I didn't want to be with people, and I couldn't bear to be alone. I wanted to know all the details, but when the Steves told me anything I wished they hadn't, and I didn't take in very much anyway. It seems silly to call them "the Steves" when they were never a couple.

It was part of the history of the club that Little Steve joined before Big Steve—and he was called Little Steve even then. It must be part of an English sense of humor to call things by their opposites, so the Surrey Downs should really be the Surrey Ups, shouldn't they? And somebody big since Robin Hood's time can only be called Little. Little Steve wasn't tall, but he was certainly big. His cock was eleven inches long—we measured it one poker night—the sort every man thinks he deserves, but it didn't bring much joy to Little Steve. It never stood properly upright. There was always a bit of a loll going on. It could have happened to any one of us. That was one of the things I was told that day, as Big Steve and Little Steve fumbled through the attempt to console me. And there was a speck of truth in it, just the smallest speck of truth. Anyone hitting that patch of oil was going to go the same way. But it was always going to be Ray who led the pack into the bend, nobody else.

It could have happened to any one of them, but it could only have happened to him.

I asked them very calmly to tell me when the funeral was, and they said they couldn't do that. I wanted to go to Cardinals Paddock, and they said it wouldn't do any good. I said I wanted to go anyway, and if they wouldn't take me I'd get there some other way. At last they gave in, even if they weren't happy about it.

I don't even remember whose back I rode behind on the way to Hampton, whether it was the bulky Steve or the wiry one inside the leather jacket in front of me. Their differences were made into nothing by the dreadful thing they shared, the fact that they were neither of them Ray. If I held on to the man in front of me, it was with no sense of human contact. In fact, though, as I remember it, I held on fiercely. I held on like grim death.

I'd always felt safe as Ray's chosen pillion, except for one time. We were on a run to Bristol—in 1979, was it?—when suddenly I got this shooting pain on one side of my chest. I realized at once this was a heart attack, and yet I said nothing. I didn't call out, I didn't try to do anything about it. It wasn't that I wanted to die. I didn't in the least want to die. But it was only the timing that was wrong. There would come a better time to die, but there could never be a better place.

Somehow Ray had realized there was something wrong, and he pulled over. I could hardly get off the bike; my knees were trembling. Ray had to hold me up. He asked me what was wrong, and I couldn't get the words out. Apparently my face was quite white. The rest of the club were pulling up and dismounting, clustering around us, half curious and half annoyed. Ray unzipped my jacket—not the horrible naff one from 1975, a proper bike jacket, a birthday present from him. I was almost collapsing, he had to support me under the arms. Then for some reason he thought of unbuttoning my shirt.

And a dead bee fell out. It must have been trapped between my shirt and my belly, and been driven to sting me, suicidally, out of confusion and despair, if bees can feel those things.

When we drew up at Cardinals Paddock, and I got off from behind whichever Steve it was that had given me a ride, I could see at once that the blinds were down in the big living-room window. Ray only ever had them that way on the Saturdays when he was playing host. I rang and rang at the bell, but of course there was no one there. Then I thought to ring the bell of the downstairs flat, which was occupied by Graham, a nice architect whose girlfriend stayed over on alternate weekends. Finally he came to the door.

Of course Graham knew something of what had happened. At this point he certainly knew more than I did. He'd always seemed to be well-disposed to us. He looked after the flower beds which I'd noticed on that first night, even though they belonged technically to a number of flats. No one else could be bothered. He even cleared away the pungent droppings the foxes left, on their eerily regular visits—every night at nine on the dot, or else at ten with the same punctuality.

I remember one Sunday morning he explained to me the symbolism of the passion flower, which produced such glorious blossoms in May and such pulpy fruit in July. He tried to show me the trinity symbolized in the flower, the four evangelists, twelve apostles, fourteen stations of the Cross faithfully mapped out in the arrangement of pistils, stamen, petals, and I just smiled and moved away, thinking he was going to ask me why he hadn't seen us in church. He can't have known I worked as a gardener. I knew about *passiflora* from a gardening angle, how they like sun and shelter, though I didn't know its meaning, if plants have a meaning. I suppose in this country the best sort of neighbor is the quiet predictable one, the one who doesn't disturb you but whose movements you know, and that made Ray a good neighbor. He was usually quiet and very predictable in his movements. It didn't matter that our ways weren't regular, as long as we were regular in our ways. You could put it like that. On poker nights, which were only at that address every couple of months, the action was occasionally rowdy and went on late, but Ray always gave fair warning. He also kept relations sweet on those occasions by leaving a drinkable present outside Graham's door—a bottle of wine or Scotch, a case of beer.

What Graham told me was that Ray's mother had already cleared out the flat. She'd made a bonfire out the back and burned a lot of papers. Graham watched her from his back window. He had wanted to retrieve something for me, he told me, anything he could rescue from the fire, but Ray's mother had fetched a stool from the kitchen and sat there keeping watch until everything was properly consumed. He couldn't see her face, but for want of a poker in the flat she used the brush from the toilet to agitate the embers. So as to be sure that nothing survived. It's the single thing I know about her, that this person could stir the ashes she had made of her son's life with a toilet brush. Ray didn't like me to say "toilet." The word he used was "lavatory."

The next day the removal van had come. It took away my clothes and my half shelf of books along with everything of Ray's. Graham let me go upstairs, which was always going to be a futile exercise. But I wasn't prepared for what I saw there: a shiny new surround for the keyhole. Ray's mother had changed the locks. Even after she'd had the flat emptied, and had burned things rather than risk throwing them away, the mother had spent good money to prevent me from using the key which the son hadn't trusted me enough to give. And that was when I got hysterical. The Steves had to pretty much carry me downstairs, and then I refused point blank to get on a motorcycle again.

I didn't even think of the trouble I was causing. Graham had to call a cab to take me home to Mum and Dad's, and when it arrived Big Steve had to travel with me, while Little Steve followed on his bike. Then from Isleworth Little Steve gave Big Steve a lift back to Hampton to pick up his own machine. A long way round for the Steves, and all because I hadn't thought.

It was only when Big Steve was putting his helmet on outside Mum and Dad's that I realized there was something fishy going on. I asked when the funeral was. I knew I'd asked that before, and the answer hadn't made any sense, so this time I made sure I caught it and kept it in my head. Again they said they couldn't tell me. And when I asked why they couldn't tell me, they said they couldn't tell me because the funeral had already happened.

It gets worse. When I asked where Ray was buried or where his ashes were, they said they couldn't tell me that either. "Couldn't tell" not meaning didn't know. Meaning weren't allowed to pass on.

Ray had sworn the whole group to silence. Sworn them not to tell me. And when had he done that? In hospital.

My mind was working very slowly. They don't take dead people to hospital. So what the Steves were saying was that Ray hadn't been killed on the spot. He'd lived long enough—

Big Steve said seventy-two hours, Little said more like forty-eight—while he was at death's door, to keep me away forever. He shut death's door against me.

It was bad enough when Ray's death was like a bolt of black lightning, but now it was a sort of death smear across several days. And I couldn't tell myself any more what I'd been telling myself since I heard: that Ray knew nothing about what had happened to him, so it didn't make a difference, except of course to me, that I wasn't there with him. Ray knew. And I wasn't there.

After that day, I fully expected my hair to go white, the way Dad's had. Except that I was almost shaven-headed, and it would have to grow in a bit before it showed. When it grew back, it was certainly thinner than before, but that's not the same thing. Maybe it's a myth that shaving hair makes it grow back stronger. I can well believe that if my hair had been long enough to notice it would have been falling out in handfuls.

It turns out that even Dad's hair, which showed such a sudden and shocking change, didn't exactly turn white. Shock causes accelerated hair loss, and what happened to him in 1975 was just that the hair with a bit of color in it tended to fall out, and the white hairs tended to stay. The hairs you want fall out, and the hairs you'd be glad to see the back of stick around. Just what you'd expect.

Mum was glad to have me back living in Isleworth full time, and not just because she liked me to have more hair than Ray had allowed. Dad was getting to be more and more of a handful, though it wasn't any easier to work out exactly what the problem was.

After France his difficulties with balance got more and more intense, even though no scan or EEG ever traced a cause. Dad stopped trusting his feet to carry him, unless he was coaxed and chivvied and supported, and it wasn't too long before Mum had to stop working too.

I'd persuaded the Steves to give me their phone numbers, and for a while I kept pestering them with pointless questions. Eventually one of them—I don't even remember which—spoke to Mum and told her it had to stop. I felt it had to stop, too. I felt the secrecy about Ray had to stop. But no, that had to stay. I had to stop calling. That was what had to stop.

It was hard for me to stop phoning them and asking them things, because they'd known Ray. And I hadn't. I didn't know what he did for a living, if he even worked. I didn't know his birthday, and since the two Steves told slightly different stories I didn't know for certain which of two days had been the date of his death. That's why I had such a desperate need to see his gravestone. To be better informed.

Wouldn't Ray have wanted to celebrate his own birthdays, if he'd known he was going to have so few of them? Rather than borrowing mine.

I didn't even know his last name. Among club members we weren't called Ray and Colin, we went by Smith and Jones. I'm Colin Smith, but I've no reason to think that Ray's last name was Jones. The odds against that would have to be astronomical, like the odds that we did actually by the wildest chance share a birthday.

Eventually I realized that Graham the downstairs neighbor was likely to know Ray's last name, if not from his own mouth then from the post that Ray made sure I never saw, but when I went, strangely fearful, back to Hampton, Graham had moved. I was almost relieved, and I didn't try to pursue him. There seemed to be a part of me that wanted not to know.

Of course I should have asked Graham on that fatal Sunday, but in fact that wasn't the great regret I had about that day. Graham could only have told me the name on Ray's mail, the name he was living under, and why would that be the one he was born with and buried by? My true regret was that I accepted Steve's lift from Box Hill to Hampton, and so forfeited the right to say that the last time I ever sat on a motorcycle I was sitting behind Ray. Breathing down his neck. If I'd just been a bit more on the ball at Box Hill, I could have kept that pledge for myself. It was something I could have controlled, and I let it go without even noticing.

The Steves thought it would comfort me to realize that it was only Ray's safety-mindedness, and the spaced-out grouping he insisted on, which ensured that no one but him went into that oil and that skid. They weren't well keyed in to my mood. Actually I felt that they had no business avoiding the oil. And as for me, by rights I should have been right behind Ray. Breathing down his neck as we slid together into the oil.

Not that I had a right to die with Ray, necessarily. But if I'd only been injured and in the same hospital as him, surely the club members would have refused to swear when Ray wanted their silence? Then I would still have had a stake in what had happened. It wouldn't have been so easy to exclude me, to separate me from what happened to him.

The year after Ray's death lasted much longer than the six before it. That's a fact. And six years is a long time for most things, too long for most things, but it wasn't a long time to spend with Ray. Then I pulled myself together somewhat, after a certain amount of feeling sorry for myself, and I got a job with London Transport. I was never meant to be a gardener, or at least a bowls-green-mowing, begonia-planting machine operated by Mikey Jarvis, a man who would happily drink the water out of flower vases, so long as the vases belonged to Princess Margaret. From the start of my training with LT, I felt I was in the right place at last. Not home, exactly, but the right place to be.

I didn't stop thinking about Ray just because a certain amount of time went by. There were changes in the world that made me daydream. I'd wonder what he would have made of them. I couldn't help thinking that he'd have loved CDs. He would have grumbled about the absurd expense, and then planned with suppressed gloating to replace all his treasured holdings. Or perhaps he would have gone the other way. I could just about imagine him sticking with vinyl, writing impassioned letters to specialist journals about tonal fidelity—wide-band response or whatever it is.

But on balance I think he would have gone with CDs. He would have loved remote controls—the ability to change the music without our needing to shift position. His legs gripping my neck, my head heavy against his crotch. Perhaps he would have invested in one of those rather unwieldy CD players with a sort of carousel that can take five discs at a time.

When the AIDS came along, that was different. Somehow I couldn't put that together with Ray in my head. He was reckless, and he was safety-conscious. There was the time on a bike run to Bristol that he took me to a pub on a collar and leash. Straight pub. And nobody turned a hair, nobody questioned his right to do as he pleased. Well, someone said "Good doggie" to me, so I bit him. All right, not bit him. Snarled a bit and snapped my teeth.

Ray was big on self-control, and he didn't know when to stop. He loved rules, and he loved to break them, that was the thing. Once he pulled over on a busy road, angled the bike to give a little cover, told me to undo my jeans, bent me over the bike and fucked me there and then. Broad daylight. He was punishing me or rewarding me for something I'd done or hadn't done, I can't remember which or what. With Ray it was best to accept him the way he was and not try too hard to make everything connect up. At least I had the choice of closing my eyes, to blot out the violation of my privacy, but I couldn't keep them shut. I don't know why.

And then while he was still hammering away, and we were both getting into a rhythm, would you believe it, a car pulled up to ask directions. I didn't want to get into the rhythm, but the rhythm was there. The man was driving and the woman was frowning as she held the map up in front of her. Car drivers seem to think bikers know every destination, or maybe it's just that there aren't windows to give bikers a bit of privacy. It must be even worse now that every other biker's a dispatch rider, and all the others are supposed to know where every little alleyway is, by magic.

Ray didn't pull out of me, but he stopped pushing long enough to set them on the right road, and they moved off. But then they only went a few yards, either because the lady had done a double take and realized what had been in front of her eyes, or because the gentleman put two and two together. From where the car is now we aren't screened, and Ray twists me round so there can be no doubt, and he starts in on me again, and he shouts, "Do you want to be after me with him, Madam?" Always polite. Most polite when being outrageous. And this time they don't hang around. Normally Ray didn't come inside me, but that time he did. Before the AIDS, nobody worried about where come went or didn't go, but there was usually a special reason for Ray to come inside me. He'd be making a point of some kind. Mischief or angry glee. Coming with a shout.

So I don't know what Ray would have done when the AIDS came along. Anyone who told him what to do was taking their life in their hands, and yet safety was almost an obsession with him. For all the good it did him on the bike. Anything he cared about was an obsession with him. I'm sure he'd have called it the AIDS, though, like I do. He cared about details, and it's logical. The S in AIDS stands for syndrome, and you wouldn't say Freddie Mercury died of syndrome, would you? *The* syndrome. Therefore, *the* AIDS.

The fact is, I can't see Ray changing his ways and using condoms, and I can't see him carrying on as before. I dare say he'd never bought a condom in his life, but maybe he would have started. Men who went with men didn't buy condoms in those days, but there's always a first time, for anyone. I try so hard to see it happening, and still I can't.

I feel guilty that I can't follow him along either of those paths to the present day. It's as if by not being able to imagine him dealing with the next set of changes, somehow I consent to his being dead, and he falls back into the past forever. It's not quite that May 1981 was the right time for him to die. More that it was nearly the last time he could live the life he'd chosen, the one he shared with me.

I don't even know whether the club carried on in some form. Some much muted form. I planned never to be on a motorcycle again, and after that day Box Hill was the last place on earth that I wanted to visit. My sense of it was that Ray was indispensable, that for all practical purposes he was the club, but the surviving members may have decided to try and make a go of it. If they did, it will have been Kevin who missed me most. If anyone missed me at all. After I stopped calling the Steves, naturally enough I lost touch. And then I had my preoccupations: Mum and Dad, and how things were going with them. How to give Mum some time off, now that Dad had stopped seeing his children as any sort of substitute for her, however temporary.

Sometimes there was something infuriating about the way Mum coped. She wouldn't allow herself to go to a film on her own (Dad wouldn't go), or even go shopping except when there was nothing in the house and I wasn't free, but she would run next door, which was just as far away in Dad's eyes, to do things for Marjorie.

Typical Mum. Her husband turns into a complete dependent and what does she do? She finds someone else who needs looking after. Marjorie next door is housebound by now and not far from blind, so Mum decides to take care of her too. Which would be fine, except that Marjorie is very "particular," and if you're trying to help her out you have to do it her way.

She'd rap on her kitchen window with her stick, and Mum would go round to see what it was she wanted. It was worse if Mum wasn't in earshot, or couldn't come right away. First Marjorie would rap softly with the rubber tip, then she'd make a bit more noise. And after five minutes she'd turn the cane round and rap sharply on the glass with its handle.

It was absurd. Mum ended up cooking separate meals for Marjorie because she was so fussy—or meals just different enough to take trouble. Same dish, different recipe. Marjorie couldn't or wouldn't eat onions (*couldn't* was her version), so Mum would make a separate little dish of stew for her. I like plain food myself, but stew without onions isn't worth the eating.

Marjorie wouldn't eat trifle, not as a finished thing. She liked everything that went into it, but something about trifle all mixed together turned her stomach. The oozing into each other of cream and juice. So Mum laid everything out side by side for Marjorie on little dishes: sponge, fruit, custard and cream. It was like a diagram of trifle. An exploded drawing of trifle. And Mum took it all next door on a tray.

It offended me that Mum let herself be used like that, but that was how she wanted it. I suppose some of my annoyance was selfish, on days when Marjorie kept banging on her kitchen window and I was trying to catch up on kip after a late turn.

At least I had that to think of. My new job. My career as a driver.

Big Steve got in touch a couple of years back. He'd kept Mum and Dad's number, and he didn't seem too surprised that I was still there. I didn't tell him then that more had changed than he might think: my little Dad had died, and so a few months later had Marjorie the neighbor. In her will she left her little house to Mum, for looking after her so well and so long. Only fair. It's more of a cottage than a house, really.

So Mum moved next door, and she sold the old house to me. To be exact: me and Simon, a mate from work. We went half and half on the mortgage. That way Mum had a bit of a nest egg, and can take holidays more or less when she wants to. The sun does her arthritis a lot of good. If she goes somewhere like Portugal she can forget to bring her cane with her from the hotel and not even notice.

So it was the same Isleworth number that Big Steve called— only the prefix had changed—but I was now the subscriber. Cosubscriber. I try to make Simon feel that our shares are really equal, even if my memories of the house go all the way back.

Once I'd got over my surprise, of course, I started pestering him all over again. I couldn't help wondering if a time period for keeping Ray's secret had passed, fifteen years or so, or if someone who was being protected had died, if that was what it was all about, so secrecy no longer mattered. Big Steve made me promise not to ask again, or he wouldn't call round the next weekend, which was what he was planning. I gave it one last try. "How can it possibly matter after all this time?" I asked, but the answer was the same one it always was. A promise is a promise.

I gave my word that I'd control myself and not bother him with pointless questions, just to be sure he'd come.

Since the last time I'd seen him, Big Steve had gained weight and lost hair. Frankly, he was bloated and bald, but that's just what happens. He rolled up on a Honda Gold Wing. Ray wouldn't have been quite so forgiving about that.

Big Steve gave me news of the group that had been. Mark had died, but in a bike crash. It's funny, when Steve told me that, I thought "natural causes." Though there's nothing natural about a motorcycle crash. A motorcycle crash is an artificial death, but diseases are part of nature. Still, up to that time at least, the AIDS hadn't touched them.

Before he left, he was keen to show off the Gold Wing. He had one of those cushions made of wooden beads—the taxi driver's friend—fastened to the saddle. The bike had heated hand-grips and a reverse gear. It was embarrassing. I mean, it wasn't that he had some great obligation to stick with British iron, though that much-loved make Triumph has made a bit of a comeback. Thanks to Japanese technology and a sophisticated computerized assembly line you can get custom features at a standard price.

I haven't climbed on a bike since 1981, but that doesn't mean I'm not allowed to read the magazines once in a while.

But if Big Steve wanted to stay on two wheels, he had to have been able to do better than a Gold Wing. It's a fat smug novelty bike—all it needs to top it off is a dog in the top box wearing a scarf, sunglasses and its own little helmet. I mean, if you want to retire from biking while still technically riding a motorcycle, you get yourself a BMW. That's something everybody knows.

All very rich, I know, coming from someone like me. Someone who's never driven anything larger than a bicycle, unless you count Tube trains.

People seem to think it's preposterous that I should be in charge of an Underground train on a daily basis when I don't have a driving license. To which I say: It's a completely different set of skills. No one ever needed to put a Tube train through a three-point turn. And in fact one of my workmates, mentioning no names, lost his license for drinking, but he's still legal driving a train. It tickles me to talk about my years "on the road," which is what we always call it, but I enjoy being a little misleading. Every trade has its quirky way of describing things.

First question I ask, if I meet another driver, is "Which line?" Which line does he drive. And it's the first thing he wants to know about me. It sounds a neutral thing to be asking, but it's as loaded as questions get. There's a tribal thing involved. All tunnels aren't alike, in fact some of them aren't exactly tunnels. So if I meet another driver away from work, he asks me which line and I say, "Circle," he knows I don't go down deep. And if I ask him and he says "District," then we can both relax and consider the possibility of a real conversation. Even Stevens. But if he says, "Central," then we're just going to circle around each other endlessly, bristling. Because I know the dismissive phrase that's on the tip of his tongue.

Okay, the Circle Line isn't like a coal mine, but we don't just scratch the surface. The gauge of the track is the same, but the bodies of our coaches are actually wider. They're serious trains.

Still, what he's thinking, and I know he's thinking it, is: that's not a Tube, that's a *cut-and-cover*. Where they just sunk in a rail bed and clapped a roof on it. Not exactly a great technical achievement. Deep-tunnel drivers can be mean-spirited little snobs.

So *I'm* thinking: we're on what was the world's first underground railway. Dug by hand, just think of that, before the invention of the Greathead Shield took the terrible risk and labor out of it. And *he's* thinking: That's not a tunnel. That's a trench with a lid.

It would be much easier for me to strike up a friendship with a bus driver, or conductor, or a ticket office worker, than with a deep-tunnel driver. We could discuss conditions of work, depots, the dreaded public, even the weather. It's not that there aren't rivalries between bus drivers and so on. I'm sure there are. It's just they wouldn't come into play. For all I know, two-man bus crews spit at single operators, and the number 11 has it in for the number 37. But I wouldn't know that, and the two of us could have a cup of tea and just chat.

So now I have a work life—not a vocation, maybe not what everyone would call a career, but more than a bare job, a work life that gives you something back. And it's only since I've had a work life of my own that I've wondered at all seriously about Ray's.

What did he do with the days? What did he do between the time he walked me downstairs before nine—sometimes a lot before nine—and the time he let me in again at six? Of course, earning their living is the main reason people have to set those hours aside. Going to work. But I'm not so sure.

Suppose that every weekday morning, after I left, Ray put

on one of the dark suits I never saw him wear, walked a few hundred yards and worked in an office. Say he was a solicitor.

Of course I've run through all the books on Ray's shelves in my mind, to see if they would fit in with his being a solicitor or anything else. But then I realize that nothing on my shelves would tell you what I do for a living. And if Ray was a solicitor, wouldn't he keep his law books in a chambers or somewhere?

But say he worked all day making people's wills and conveyancing. When did he do his wrestling and his martial arts? When was there time for that? Ray wasn't an amateur—well of course he was an *amateur*, but he wasn't a dabbler.

Three times a week I put on the washing machine in the kitchen, and his kit was in it either once or twice. When I lifted it from the laundry basket, it held the smell of his sweat, the unmistakable savory tang with its underwhiff of honey. If there's one smell in the world I'm qualified to authenticate, it's Ray's sweat. Once I asked him, "Did you have a good session?" and he answered, "It's called a workout" so coldly that I never asked again.

But if you go at it the other way round, the picture makes no more sense. If Ray didn't need to work, if Ray had money, then how did he spend his time? Did he sit around in a dressing gown, make a phone call to his banker, then take a cab into the West End for lunch? It's a chilling idea to me that he might have had a world of friends who knew nothing of the bike club, just as we knew nothing of them. Perhaps there was a bridge session, on a Wednesday afternoon, as well as poker night on a Saturday. It's enough to give you nightmares.

In theory it would have been possible for him to work three or four days, and still have a serious martial arts workout a couple of times a week, but that sort of balance doesn't seem to tell the truth about the man. His life wasn't about either responsibility or leisure. What I saw of his life was about excitement, about magic. About casting a spell.

If I'd dared to spy on him, all those years ago, I wouldn't be living with so much uncertainty now. It wouldn't have been an elaborate surveillance project, as such things go, to watch Cardinals Paddock from four o'clock if only one afternoon, to see if he came back after that time, and if so what he was wearing, before he came clattering down the stairs at six in his leathers to let me in. True, Hampton isn't a bustling place; it would have been quite a feat to lie low. But I never even thought about it. If Ray could know I was looking down at him while he washed the bike without needing to use his eyes, I could be sure he would detect any ruse of mine, and would certainly punish it— not the sort of punishment that's like a reward in reverse, but an absolute cutting off, leaving me to regret my curiosity for the rest of my life. Leaving me to curse myself for not leaving things alone. It would only have taken a little initiative to find out more about Ray, but that wasn't my department. Initiative was Ray's department.

I wonder how much time he spent wondering what was going on in my head, in the six years we had together, compared to the amount of time I've spent since then wondering what was going on in his. I freely admit I have no idea what it was like for him to lead the bike club on a run in its convoy of menace and glitter. Knowing that everyone was too impressed by him even to feel jealous. I was right behind in the formation. Breathing down his neck. But I know as little as any.

So I tell myself that Ray couldn't imagine what it's like for me to take a train into a station. A driver is there in the cab for the public to see, and be reassured. It could all be automated, like

94

the Docklands Light Railway, but even there the public wants to see a face. And if they can see us, we can see them.

I had someone on the track my first day on the road. He didn't jump, but then he didn't need to jump to get my attention. He slipped down from the platform onto the track like someone slipping into the deep end of a swimming pool. Then he seemed to abase himself on the railbed. He groveled there in front of the death that was rushing slowly towards him. Of course I'd put all the anchors on, but I knew I wouldn't be able to stop in the time I had, the space I had. It had already happened. My *first* day on the road.

And then he swam up again, scrambled up to the platform surface, and was gone. I of course was in shock, and wandered blankly out of my cab and down the platform. All I could think of was that a suicide had changed his mind or some pranny had done it for a bet. So I was trying to hold both reactions in my mind at the same time, relief and anger, until I could find out which was the one to suppress and which the one to let loose. When a couple of people told me what had happened, I still didn't know what the right reaction was. What to hold in, what to let out.

It was only a commuter who'd dropped his ticket and nipped down by the live rail to pick it up. That's the sort of thing we're dealing with. Then he ran off, to avoid getting a piece of my mind, but perhaps he was lurking just out of sight, waiting for me to get back in my cab so he could sneak back onto the platform, with the smuts on his suit and the rat droppings on his shoes, to resume his interrupted journey. The journey he'd interrupted because his pea brain couldn't tell him what was important and what was not.

That was my first customer on the line. I've been lucky. We

drivers don't deal direct with the public, so in fact we haven't been trained to use the new words that we hear on the tannoy: "customers" until they're actually on the track, and then for some reason they're "passengers." A passenger incident at Marble Arch. I was joking about it with a mate at work, saying that it was mad that they became passengers just when they weren't going anywhere, and he said with a straight face that he thought it was the right word. Anybody else, you don't know where they're going really, but the ones on the track have arrived. They've gone as far as they're going to go.

So far there's only been one more in front of my cab, and I haven't seen a death. I've been lucky. Still, after the first one, you look out of your grimy window a little differently. If my own little Mum was on the platform waving at me I wouldn't really take it in. I'm braced for whatever the track has to show me. I'm not moving at any speed, but then nor was Ray. Speed isn't the only factor.

Number Two couldn't have been more different from Number One, the ticket collector. This was at Paddington. She wasn't waiting on the platform. There wasn't much of a crowd; it wasn't rush hour. She must have worked out her timing, waiting for the thunder of my train, before she set off. Then she pounded up the stairs, and leaped to end her life.

It's just that she underestimated her fitness, or even her desperation. What I saw from behind my grimy glass was a person sailing from right to left, and keeping on going. I could see her smart blouse and her running shoes, the shoes she wore to make sure she didn't slip before she leaped. She would have crashed into the wall and then been crushed against it by my train, except that at Paddington there are two tracks side by side. She sailed right past me, past my train, and broke her ankle in perfect safety on the other track.

Of course, we had to make sure we got her off there before the next train came along. In fact it isn't the true suicides we drivers are haunted by. Yes, they're selfish to use our trains for their purposes, to involve us by making us watch. And commuters get vexed. But sooner or later they'll find their way to what they want, if only they want it enough. It's different with the casuals. That's where the trauma lies, for us. When it didn't need to happen. One lad who started on the road at the same time as me was never the same after a casual. City gent. Father of three. Sees the lace of his handmade shoe is undone. Bends down to tie it up. Not realizing that his shoe is safe where it is. But his head. In its new position. Is not.

There's a thought about Ray I've been having for a while now. I've been trying it on in my head to see how it feels. It's a thought about Thursdays. Not weekdays in general. Just Thursdays.

I wasn't trusted to clean Ray's bike, though you might think it was just the sort of careful maintenance work I was suited for. Still, Ray had his cleaning ritual. I wasn't even trusted to oil his leathers, or to run the candle stubs every week or so along the zips to keep them fluent. True, I was trusted to clean his bike boots, but that was a little different. He kept them on. He liked broad preparatory strokes, with me using my tongue at its widest, like a paintbrush, before he signaled that I could start with the brushes and the polish.

So the question is: was I unworthy, or was it that Ray found it hard to let go of certain things? And the follow-up question is the troubling one: if Ray couldn't delegate cleaning the bike to someone he shared his life with and who would have felt privileged to do it, how could he bear to let a stranger into his private space once a week to clean up?

If you want something done properly, do it yourself. If that really was Ray's philosophy, then perhaps I've found the second point of tallying between him and my little Dad. That was Dad all over, but only Dad before 1975. The Dad who brought me up, not the Dad who came later.

I'm trying to get used to the idea that there wasn't anybody letting themselves in on a Thursday to do housework. That the household was simpler than I thought, but also more complicated. If I was the houseboy, as I suppose you'd say, Ray was the cleaning lady. If I was the footstool, still, he changed the black sheets on the bed where he slept. I made the bed, and I'd better do it neatly, but once a week it was his turn. He changed the linen and plumped the pillows his head would rest on.

It ought to be a horrible idea, but there's something about it that fits better than my imagination of a solicitor or a rich kid. It makes me look at my life with him in a new way. The price I pay for that is having to imagine Ray cleaning the toilet's throat with the brush that his mother used, after he died, to make sure that nothing remained of his life.

I always made out to myself that what happened on Box Hill in 1975, on my eighteenth birthday, was beyond my control. As if I was one of those kidnap victims who become obsessed with their captors—just that it happened very quickly, thanks to Ray's charisma, so that everything was already decided by the time I first got on the bike behind him.

Well, Ray's charisma was real, and I wasn't the only to feel it. But I went along with it. It's only exaggerating a little to say that I knew what I was doing when I fell over those long and insolently extended legs. I was ready. I had no real idea of what I was ready for, but still I was ready.

Even sudden things have a history behind them. Maybe it's the sudden things that have the most history. Sooner or later I was going to have to respond to excitement and danger. It was just a question of when and how I was going to do it. Sooner or later I was going to have to answer the call of the live rail.

But when I did, it turned out I was braver than I thought. I wasn't like the man who slipped down there, too stupid to be parted from his ticket, my first day on the road. I was as unhesitating as that other jumper, the one who sailed right past the risk and landed on the far side of it, relieved, disappointed and with absolutely no idea what was going to happen next. I didn't even break an ankle.

A couple of years ago I took my nephew Charlie up to London. Half-term treat. He was the baby that stopped Joyce from going on holiday in 1981, the pregnancy. But you can't hold a grudge. Particularly as for a while yet he still thinks it's cool to have an uncle that drives trains. We ended up in Whitehall, at Horse Guards. We'd spent the afternoon watching roller skaters hurtling around in a theater, pretending to be trains, and here was stillness. The Guards looked out from under their helmets as if the space was empty for miles in front of them, as if the other side of Whitehall was a white desert stretching far beyond the Thames. Charlie was fascinated, and seemed to want me to try and catch their eyes, by shouting or clapping or waving my arms, though he was reaching an age to be mortified if I had. He was at that stage when kids are trying to teach themselves to slouch and look surly, but he kept straightening up, watching the Horse Guards, his posture improving by leaps and bounds until he caught himself and forced himself to slouch all over again.

The Horse Guards reminded me of Ray, of course. Being ignored has always stirred me up somehow. I feel unworthy, naturally, but I'm also tuned up by it, as if a change was suddenly going to come over this handsome blank of a face that won't look at me, and when it does I will respond immediately and without question. As if a man is only a man if he takes no notice of me.

You could say the Horse Guards reminded me of Ray. Or you could say Ray reminded me of the Horse Guards, as I saw them when it was me that was the schoolboy at half term. How far do you have to go back to understand how something started? Maybe Ray was a substitute for something, but still. There was no substitute for Ray.

The Sound of Music was the show to see then, not *Starlight Express*, but it was always Whitehall and the Horse Guards. Charlie said he wanted to go to the London Dungeon, but I think that's unhealthy, and anyway I told him London Bridge was too far from Victoria, where the show was. When I suggested the Horse Guards, and told him there were real horses, he brightened up.

In fact you could call today's Horse Guards only rigid and unresponding by comparing them to the watching crowds who slouch and shuffle round them. If you look closely, you can see all sorts of little fidgets. The Horse Guards I remember as a schoolboy were fidget-proof, and you could really believe they were going to faint before they'd blink. Each one of them was a unit with no subordinate parts, and they would either sit their horses unmoving or fall from the saddle as a single mass.

I'm not saying the old style was better, I'm just stating a fact, that a change has taken place. And it's not particularly that I'm affected by the changes in me, now that I'm looking at a soldier who's half my age and not twice as old as me. The Horse Guards used to look as if they were stone, and now they're only fiberglass. A strong wind would blow them down. I don't even regret the difference, it's just that the whole ritual begins to look silly, now that soldiers can't manage the discipline, that really mad level of self-control. Better to scrap it.

It's a change of attitude. People don't think it's marvelous that the Queen sits so still on her horse for Trooping the Color. It's not just that she's not a young woman any more, and that they wonder if her bottom is getting sore. They don't think what they used to think, that as long as we can do pageantry better than anyone in the world we can hold our heads up. They think, Doesn't she have something better to do on her birthday? Even if it is only her official one. We all know about her love of horses and her sense of duty, but if she had a birthday wish it might just be to Troop the Color from the comfort of a golf cart.

It was a long time after Ray that I even tried to get back into the swim of things. The swim of sex. In a way it's much simpler these day, what with the phone lines, but I can't help feeling it's still always going to be a bit hit-and-miss. One fellow I was talking to asked my weight, and when I told him what it was he said it wasn't going to work, and hung up. Fair enough. But he obviously felt bad about it. He phoned up again and said he'd felt rotten about hanging up. Nice fellow. I told him not to worry, I'm used to it. I don't even mind. Being pear-shaped is fine, but only if you're a pear. Then I suggested maybe I could wear a T-shirt, cover up a bit. So he said, Good idea, we can try that. And we did, and it was fine. But there wasn't that spark.

Not everyone is so straightforward, even on the phone when you can just hang up if things aren't working. One man wanted me to visit him in Milton Keynes, gave me his mobile number and everything. Then when I'd got to the address he'd told me, it was a warehouse and his mobile was turned off. It wasn't an expensive trip, thanks to the travel concessions that go with being on the road, but he wasn't to know that. And it took five hours out of my life. One of these days he'll switch his mobile phone on again, and I'll give him a piece of my mind.

Another chap, ex-squaddie, had the strength in the legs that was bound to appeal to me. Years since I had a good squeeze. Only thing was, he called me names. Dog, pig, slave. I don't like to be called names. Still, if he called again I expect I'd put up with it. Maybe drop a hint that it doesn't do a lot for me. Less than nothing, really.

I'm not comfortable on my knees any more, for longer than a few minutes—I had an ulcerated leg a year ago, and it's still not right. So I brought along some kneepads, not the biker sort but the ones decorators wear when they're doing some sanding. So that my knees don't let me down.

I'm bolder with my eyes since Ray. If there's something in front of me that I like, I'll look at it squarely. It may be a biker. If it is, he probably won't be wearing the neon shades of leather that are the style now. It's likely to be black. I'm old-fashioned that way, though I have a little bit of a soft spot for the green-and-white Kawasaki colors. And if the biker wearing the black leather says, "What are you looking at?" I'll just say, "If you don't want me looking, wear something else." Not just in my head but out loud. It's as simple as that.

If it's not a biker, then it's a sort of careless strength that speaks to me. It might be someone on a building site pushing a wheelbarrow, heading towards a plank balanced against a skip. He can't hesitate if he's going to get his load safely up the plank, but he doesn't want the wheel to jar against the beginning of the plank. So what he does, the moment before he gets there he presses down hard from the shoulders. Just for a second, but it's enough to compress the tire. Then when he releases the pressure and it rebounds, the barrow bounces up onto the plank right on cue. I love to see that.

Ray was good to me—he was. He even kept the promise he made, without using words, the night we met. He didn't fuck anyone else in those six years. Fucking meaning actually fucking. You could say he was faithful, and he was good to me. But I could never have loved someone who was only ever good to me. That was true before I met him and it's still true now.

This year Mum and I went on an outing that ended in a place I didn't expect. It was soon after my birthday, my forty-second. Normally I don't have much free time, but one of my classes hadn't materialized. It's maddening when that happens. I'd done all the preparation. But the rules of the WEA—that's Workers' Education Association—are strict. You need six people to justify a class, and if only five turn up, even if one of them swears blind his cousin can make it every other week without fail except this one, then that's just too bad. You can wait ten minutes after the class is due to start, hoping some humble angel will turn up late and save the day, but after that you have to send them home. Trying only to feel sorry for them, and not for yourself. Romanesque architecture, too. One of my favorites. Something I love to teach.

There are few things I've wished for more strongly than for that sixth person to come through the door. But there it is. So

I had more free time this year than I'm used to. I was on leave covers, waiting to be told what my shifts were, but that way I always get a little notice of when I'll be free.

I hadn't even asked where we were driving. Mum loves to potter, she loves junk shops and car boot sales, even though she only buys something once in a blue moon. She went to a flea market the day after she came out of hospital in 1975, in a borrowed wheelchair. They didn't have car boot sales then, or they weren't called that.

And every now and then she likes a browse round a stately home. I always encourage her to get out of the house. For a while after Dad died she'd lost the habit of having a life of her own, let alone the habit of enjoying herself, but now she's got what she calls her bits and pieces. The things she likes to do. It was almost worse when Marjorie died than when Dad did. She clung to that last excuse not to live for herself.

Mum told me the name of the house when we were in the car, Polesden Lacey, and if I'm honest it rang some kind of bell, but I didn't think anything about it.

It was only when I realized we were getting close to Leatherhead that I twigged: the house is only a few miles from Box Hill. They're even closer, for instance, than Hampton is to Isleworth. But I managed to put it out of my mind. This was supposed to be Mum's day.

We've always got on well, Mum and I, even if it's only since Dad died that she said she knew I was gay and it was fine with her, as long as I was happy. Love is love, is what she said. I don't think there was a real reason why she couldn't say so with Dad alive, but all the same it would never have happened. Then the first Christmas after he died, taking some mince pies out of the oven, she just comes out with it.

I was carving crosses into the bottoms of some brussels sprouts, you know, so that the stalk bit cooks as quickly as the floret, and it wasn't really a discussion. It was more like part of Mum's Christmas list of things to do. One step up from last-minute cards, the ones you send when you get ones you hadn't expected, even though your one won't get there in time for the day and looks like the embarrassed gesture it is. Stuff the turkey. Tell Colin I know he's gay and it's fine. Tell him love is love.

Her last years with Dad were more like being under house arrest than like being married, and it's only now that she's beginning to recover, and to realize that she has a freedom, like it or not. There was never anything actually the matter with Dad. Of course, his powers started to fail when he stopped using them, but there was never a physical reason for him to do that.

I tell a lie: Dad's eyes got very dry when he got older, and I remember Mum would put artificial tears in his eyes for him. He'd grab hold of the arm that held the dropper, for some reason, and forget to let go, so Mum would gently peel the fingers back, one by one, until she was free.

We parked as near to the house as we could. Polesden Lacey isn't a great house, not especially old nor stately in any real sense, but it's a popular attraction, being so near to London, and at weekends I'm sure it's crawling with connoisseurs. The house was completed in 1824, but Mum told me that the National Trust have the rooms furnished in Edwardian style. Mum's been reading up, Mum's been doing research. It turns out that the Queen Mother spent part of her honeymoon in the house, as Duchess of York, as a guest of the Greville family who lived there then.

Mum's doctor has told her he'd classify her as disabled like a shot, but she'd see that as giving up, until the time comes that she doesn't have a choice. Till then she won't go near the disabled spaces, even though she knows I'd be happy to have a word with the parking attendants.

Mum's walking is slow, even with her stick, and she doesn't like to feel she's slowing anyone else down. So we'd agreed ahead of time that I'd ramble round the grounds, and she'd just ruminate through the house. Then we'd meet up again in the tea room at our leisure. Mum loves good silver, old silver you can gaze at as long as you like and never needs polishing, at least by you.

I expect I'm a bit the same about gardens. I can really quite enjoy them, as long as there's no possibility of being asked to pick up so much as a pair of shears. This year they're doing up the East Elevation, so I don't expect the house was looking its best—lots of scaffolding.

I wandered through the Rose Garden but it was too early for roses. There were only labels. I wonder if they named the rose Dorothy Perkins after the shop, or the shop after the rose, or both of them after something else altogether that used to be famous and isn't any more. I noticed that there was a yew hedge in the walled garden that looked very stark and one-sided, so I read the notice next to it: *One side of yew hedging will be sliced back to the main trunk. This will enable new and vigorous regeneration to take place. During establishment of the new growth, the yew stems will appear unsightly—we have to be cruel to be kind! We ask our keen and understanding garden-loving supporters to tolerate the initial period of regrowth.* The other visitors to the garden, not that there were all that many, seemed very knowledgeable about plants, Latin names and all. It seemed pathetic that I'd worked as a gardener for years and had learned so little.

I walked as far as the Thatched Bridge and then doubled back. My leg still isn't right, and I was thinking of heading for the tea room and a sit down. I took what looked like a short cut in the direction I wanted, passing through what was almost a tunnel in the bushes. Branches came down almost to my head height. Then I stopped short.

What I was looking at was row after row of little graves. A tiny churchyard. All of the graves had the full set: name, date of birth and death—*26 February 1908–30 Jan 1924* was one—and tender inscriptions. Ever-lively companion … mourn his loss. The works.

It was a bad moment for me, and even a few years ago I'd have found it shattering, to realize that the Grevilles had a cemetery for their *dogs.* Seventeen of them. For Caesar, for Tyke, for Prince Chang and the rest. For the dog with the most sweetly stabbing name of all, the West Highlander known as Little Fidelity. The Grevilles had seventeen graves to visit when they missed their dogs. And I have nowhere to visit when I want to remember Ray. With the scanty information I have, I might have seen his gravestone already and not have known it.

If Ray had died in a plane crash, if he'd been shredded and scattered, I'd be in a better position than I am, because I'd know there was no help for it. I'd understand the reasons. And nobody would be any better off than me, there'd be nobody keeping a secret. But knowing I'm the only one to be kept in the dark makes it feel like it's me that's been singled out for shredding and scattering.

That was when I decided. After I saw the dogs' cemetery. I checked the tea room first, in case Mum had tired early and gone for some refreshment, and then I paid the extra three quid to go inside the house and retrieve her. I told her I'd like to have tea somewhere else, if she didn't mind, at Box Hill. Box Hill where the bikers used to go on a Sunday. And still do I expect, only it's no one I know.

The drive took only ten minutes, between one National Trust property and another. Two treasures of different types. There's no antique silver and no rose garden at Box Hill, but there's no doubt it's the more important asset. It's been a beauty spot for centuries, it's in books, it's in paintings, there were a million visitors last year. Box Hill came to the National Trust thirty years before the Grevilles let go of Polesden Lacey.

I'd always thought that I would need to visit the place where Ray died, the bend and the tree on the B337, to finish things between us. At least I have a rough address for that moment in his life. I'd been thinking of asking Simon who shares the house to drive me one weekend, except I've not said a great deal to him about Ray, so it might seem strange.

A few weeks ago he was up in the attic and he found the martial arts magazines that I'd taken from Cardinals Paddock as a way of getting a little shelf room there. He took it for granted I'd want them throwing out, but I couldn't do it. Even though they were yellowed with age—it looked as if the years had peed on them, and still I couldn't let them go, having nothing else. And Simon had the kindness not to ask me why not.

He's even helped in the past when he really didn't know or care what it was all about. It's a mistake to think that friends need to know everything about each other. Simon did the driving when I wanted to take some pictures for a class, of a unique little church that I'd mentioned in class often enough but never actually visited, God forgive me. Greensted Green in Essex, which pioneered the parish system before there were even parishes. What I mean is, the lord of the manor moved away and the church had to organize its survival on a new basis. So an interesting place in terms of church history, quite apart from architectural merit.

Simon drove, and then lay on a convenient bench in the churchyard sleeping off the pub lunch that had been the reward for his trouble. Completely uninterested in what I was goggling at and taking pictures of, a nave built of Saxon oak, simply split tree trunks set side by side, with long tongues of wood fitting in grooves between them to seal the gaps. The oldest wooden building standing in Europe, the oldest wooden church in the world. Not to mention a picturesque churchyard, bees going about their business, bushes in flower and berry, a crusader's tomb with a low railing round it. He couldn't care less, bless him.

But it wasn't going to be Simon helping me with my past, it was going to be Mum, even if she was too tactful to mention Ray's name. Mum and I didn't talk much on the drive to Box Hill, and perhaps it wasn't quite like our usual companionable silences. I was thinking that I'd told Mum too early that widowhood was not going to be the worst part of her life, that she owed it to herself to have a good time. It sounded heartless, it sounded disloyal, but it was the truth. It wasn't going to be the worst part of her life because the worst was over—the second half of her marriage.

We've never talked about the reasons for Dad's stubborn decline over twenty years. Perhaps it'll be my turn this Christmas to open and close a huge subject in a single conversation. Perhaps while I'm sticking cards on the picture rail and the mantelpiece, and Mum lays out crackers on side plates, I'll say, "You know what happened to Dad, don't you?"

Because it's not complicated. When my little Dad stood up

on his wedding day and said he took this woman till death did them part, he was only thinking of one way that could happen. He was eleven years older, he thought he was safe. Death would take him and leave her, to manage on her own. That would never happen to him.

Then when Mum went to hospital in 1975, he suddenly realized it didn't need to be like that. She might die, and he be left. He never really recovered from the knowledge of that moment. He was a changed man. He didn't decide to die, exactly, but he was determined to get his dying in first, to stay safe and not face life without her. Never mind that from that day on he did something worse, before he widowed her.

With any luck all I'll need to say will be, "You know what happened to Dad, don't you?" and she'll say, without even looking up, "Yes, he needed to be the one who died first," and then we'll just get on with Christmas.

So on the way to Box Hill in Mum's car I was bound to be preoccupied with the past, but it may also be that she was thinking of her own problems. We both know this will be her last year driving, before her arthritis shuts down that part of her life. It's only a short time since she started to have a little freedom again, but she's cheerful about it. She even says she's looking forward to selling the car and getting an electric buggy to take her to the shops. That's silly, of course. All very valiant, but she knows I'd do her shopping for her. Having a son next door, let alone a son she calls her bestest and only, she won't be short of help. And Simon who shares the house is always offering to help. In fact he's over there so often, seeing if anything needs fixing, that I wonder if it's not him that needs the company.

It's trips like these she'll miss. It took me a long time to get her out of the house after Dad died. She'd got out of the habit.

It was as if she'd been infected over the years by his fear of the world outside. I had to take drastic measures to break her isolation. Then when she told me there was this club she wanted to join, it would give her a bit of a social life, only she couldn't face it unless I joined too, I felt I couldn't say no, even though it's pretty embarrassing.

I can cope with being called Brainiac at work, with being asked the meanings of fancy words, and to help with application forms and difficult letters, but I'm not sure I could live with it if word got out. It's bad enough being a self-taught late learner, that's an opsimath and an autodidact, without your workmates knowing the shameful truth. That you have a membership of Mensa, not only that but you share it with your Mum. Well, they've a reduced rate for people who share an address, and she does only live next door, so it seemed silly not to go for that option. It's in our names jointly, but the bumf comes to her address.

By rights I should take the summer to get my driving license, but Mum says I mustn't unless I actually want the car for myself. I know she doesn't hide things from me, and I've learned to take what she says at face value. I haven't quite made up my mind. But for myself, personally, what use do I have for a car?

There were only a few bikes by Ryka's the café at the bottom of the hill. Ryka's for bikers. I directed Mum up the approach to the Zigzag. The curves are sharp even for four-wheeled transport, vehicles you don't have to balance. They've put speed bumps down since 1981. Ray lived and died before traffic calming measures. He lived and died before car alarms that get skittish in windy weather and scream the place down. I wonder what he'd have made of those. I can imagine him riding close to parked cars—close but still safe—just to set them off.

We stopped at the top of the hill, by the servery and the shop and the information center. Mum didn't have to pay to park, thanks to being a member of the National Trust, but I noticed there was no reduction for motorbikes. They have to pay the full £1.50 to Pay and Display, which seems steep, steep as the hill itself. I gave the parking attendant a bit of a grilling about that. What he said was, We don't discriminate, which I thought was a bit dishonest. Is it discrimination to let kids under five ride my Tube for free? Discriminating is just what they're doing by making out that two different things are the same. But I kept my mouth shut. The attendant pointed out a bit defensively that there's a special grassy area for bikes, so they don't have to take their chances on loose gravel.

All very well, but it's clear what's really going on. The Trust doesn't like the ruffians who gather lower down the Hill. The Trust will do all it can to keep riffraff away from the Information Center and Shop. In the pamphlets they sell at the Shop they'll tell you about the several protected species of bat that have colonized the underground chambers of the fort near the Center, but nothing about the bikers who have colonized the place above ground. They lower the tone. That's what the pamphlet really means, when it says that "special care is needed to protect the natural beauty of the hill." Bikers push off.

Mum sat down at a picnic table while I queued for my tea and Mum's coffee. I had a chat with the lady who was working in the Servery. I came clean about my biker past. She told me that these days the approach to the hill, the A24 from Givons Grove roundabout, is heavily policed on a Sunday, to prevent racing. There used to be a lot of racing on that stretch, a lot of boy racer and speed merchant activity. Not only do they patrol heavily, but Surrey County Council recently voted on a motion to ban bikes from the hill altogether. Box Hill without the bikers on Sunday, it's impossible to imagine. The motion was voted down, but the antibike forces are sure to try again. I wonder how Ryka's Caff will deal to the threat to its livelihood. I can't see them taking it lying down.

Mum left half her coffee. She's particular about coffee. The Servery at Box Hill won the Trust's 1997 award for most hygienic food preparation environment. Now, according to mum, all they have to do is make their hygienically prepared coffee taste of something nice.

I suggested we drove a bit further on, to see if there was another place that would do a better cup. We kept on going, past the panorama, where people have looked down from the Downs for hundreds of years. Mum asked if I wanted to get out for a look—she'd stay in the car—but I said no. That wasn't the kind of perspective I was hoping to get from this day.

I could have looked for the actual tree that Ray had been leaning against all those years ago, but that wasn't something I needed either. Ray might have had his ashes scattered at the foot of that very tree, and I would never know it. I have to make my own peace. The leaves of the box are ovate, entire, smooth, thick, coriaceous and dark green, ovate meaning egg-shaped. Entire meaning undivided. Coriaceous meaning leatherlike. I looked that one up. Leaves that look or feel like leather.

I'm forced back on the only theory that makes sense, that explains why I had to lose Ray so completely when he died. He was the son of a great family. He lived his life in defiance of his station, but he couldn't stop the suffocating world he'd rejected from taking him back when he died, to the grand tomb of his ancestors. Tomb or vault. Grave with a low railing, whatever.

To the right of the road, past the panorama, we saw a pub

that offered cream teas in an annex. Mum knows I like a cream tea, and she pulled in. The pub was called Boxhills. There was a sign fixed to the fence by where we parked, announcing it as the highest tavern in Surrey.

While we waited for our order to be brought, I tried to work out why I didn't remember this pub from 1975, although I did seem to remember the sign on the fence. My memory is fairly reliable, and it bothered me that I couldn't make the sum add up. Then I realized that this wasn't a pub at all back then. Back then this was a Wimpy Bar. This was the Wimpy Bar where I ate my burger after leaving Ted to booze, all those years ago, just before I met Ray.

And there was a reason for me to remember the Surrey's Highest Tavern sign, hanging in a place I didn't recognize. It didn't used to be here. It used to be displayed outside the Hand in Hand down the road, where Ted did his boozing that day. Of course there's not much point in keeping the sign when you've lost the title—though there can only be a few inches in it. I wonder if there was a bitter wrangle between the rival landlords in the middle of Box Hill Road, or maybe a tipsy little procession and a mock-earnest ceremony of handing over the sign and the title.

You wouldn't think people would care about the height above sea level of a pub, one way or the other. It's hard to imagine someone saying, "Let's have a jar in the Hand in Hand," and his mate saying, "No, let's go to Boxhills, it's higher—it's the highest tavern in Surrey." But people can care about anything.